SO-AXR-300

# Mystery of the Fleeing Girl

(Original title: Journey with a Secret)

by SHOWELL STYLES

Illustrated by Dom Lupo

SCHOLASTIC BOOK SERVICES

NEW YORK • TORONTO • LONDON • AUCKLAND • SYDNEY

Copyright © 1969 by Showell Styles. This edition is published by Scholastic Book Services, a division of Scholastic Magazines, Inc., by arrangement with Meredith Press, original publishers of the book under the title JOURNEY WITH A SECRET.

1st printing ................................................................. March 1970
Printed in the U.S.A.

# CONTENTS

# Prologue

THE GIRL stepped out of the side door and closed it behind her as quietly as she could. She was in an alley between two tall houses, lit only by the dull glow of the London sky at midnight. The air felt warm for October but a thin drizzle of rain was falling out of the darkness, and she set down the knapsack she was carrying to pull the hood of her ski jacket over her fair hair. Her fingers were trembling so violently that she could hardly tie the nylon strings. Then, for a quarter of a minute, she stood quite still, listening.

The ceaseless hum of the city was in her ears, but the street at the end of the alley a few paces away was quiet — no footsteps, no sound of cars. At this time of night she had a good chance of crossing it and reaching the narrow side street almost opposite without being seen. She took a deep breath, picked up her knapsack, and walked quickly toward the alley's end.

The noise of a speeding car rose just as she reached the pavement. Before she could step back into the alley the headlights were sweeping around the corner thirty yards away. The blue light on the roof told her it was a police car. The tires skidded, as it drew up with a jerk at the curb, and two uniformed policemen sprang out; one of them went at once to the front door of the house she had just left and pressed the bell. The headlights were switched off now, and the girl summoned her courage and started to cross the road.

A third man had got out of the car on the side away from the pavement.

"Second floor, Sergeant," he snapped from a few feet away as she passed him. "Phillips, find the side door and stay by it — Excuse me, miss!" He took a quick stride and laid a hand gently but firmly on the girl's arm. "Didn't you come out of this house a moment ago?"

She turned to face him. He was a tall thin man in a raincoat and a soft hat. She couldn't see his eyes under the brim of the hat, but she could feel them on her as bright and pitiless as the beam of the headlights. With a tremendous effort she made herself speak.

"What house? Who are you, stopping me like this?"

"Inspector Fosdyke, C.I.D. The house the sergeant's going into now. Have you just come out of it?"

She managed to laugh. "Why should I? I don't even know who lives there."

"Oh. Where do you live, may I ask?"

"Right at the far end of this street. Number . . . number two-three-seven."

"I see."

The C.I.D. man hadn't failed to notice the slight hesitation. It might be natural nervousness, of course; he hadn't actually seen her come out of the house. There was enough light from the brightly lit road at the end of the street to show the girl's appearance clearly, and his trained eye had already recorded it: five foot four, slim, about fifteen, black or navy jacket and ski pants, small knapsack slung over shoulder, skiing boots.

"And where might you be going at this

hour?" he asked. "It's after midnight, you know."

It was on the tip of the girl's tongue to say "home," but she remembered just in time that she was heading away from number two-three-seven.

"I'm starting my holiday," she said rapidly. "I've got a train to catch and I'm late. Will you loose my arm, please?"

The Inspector took his hand from her arm but kept his eyes steadily on her. "Holiday?" he repeated, frowning.

"Yes — school holiday. I'm going youth hosteling, in . . . in Yorkshire. And my train goes at a quarter to one, so . . ."

Another car, a police ambulance this time, came rocking around the corner. It pulled up behind the police car. Its arrival had drawn Inspector Fosdyke's attention from the girl, and when he turned to continue his questioning he was just in time to see her disappearing at a run into the narrow side street across the road. He made as though to start in chase of her and then stopped himself. Ten to one a youngster like that had nothing to do with the business he had come to investigate, which was extremely urgent — a 999 call from this house, hysterical housekeeper reporting her employer stabbed to death in his study. The Inspector felt pretty sure the girl had been lying; but that didn't alter the fact that he ought to be inside the house at this moment, getting on with his investigation. He stepped to the pavement and went in through the open door, with the doctor and two ambulance men at his heels.

The rain-wet pavements were deserted, glistening in the light of the street lamps. The only man in sight now was the driver of the police car, and he was surreptitiously lighting a cigarette. He did not see the dark figure that glided from the shelter of a doorway a little farther down the street and flitted across the road like a shadow. It was the figure of a little man in a cloth cap and a short jacket with the collar buttoned over his chin. Noiselessly he gained the corner of the narrow side street and vanished into it as swiftly as the girl had.

# Police at Camp Two

"WE'RE bang on the beeline," John said; he was peering at the map by the glow from the campfire. "That's pretty average good, in my opinion."

"It's a really choice campsite, anyway," said his sister from inside the tent.

Ann Davies was thirteen, a year and a half younger than John, and "choice" was her highest praise for anything, just as John's was "pretty average good." The campsite deserved it. From where she sat with her down sleeping bag huddled around her she saw the view framed in the open doorway of the tent, and though twilight had drowned all the autumn colors, it was still very beautiful. Just outside was the bright red of the smoldering embers, with John's intent face reflecting the glow. Beyond, the depths of the wooded valley curled darkly beneath steep purple-blue hills, with here and there a tiny point of yellow light showing where the farmhouses stood. The crests of the hills were rounded black humps against a sky of greeny-blue, clear as glass, and one or two stars were beginning to twinkle in the east now that the orange tints left by the sunset were fading in the west. The air was perfectly still, and quite warm although it was October.

"We're in Wales, all right." John broke a silence which had held only the hushed murmur of the river far below. "Four miles inside the border. Fifteen miles on Saturday, sixteen today. We're doing nicely."

"How far now to the sea?" asked Ann, more because John liked calculating than because she wanted to know.

John muttered to himself for a few seconds with the map close to the fire glow and his nose close to the map.

"Just about thirty-seven," he said at last, "but that's not including any detours. Two more camps and we're there."

"Let's hope they're as nice as Camp Two,"

Ann said. "And that the weather keeps on like this."

It had been John's idea to spend the week of the autumn holiday making a beeline walk to the sea, and Ann — who was as interested in camping and hill walking as her brother — had agreed enthusiastically. Their home was near the Shropshire-Staffordshire border, and John had worked out that by walking due west in a straight line for sixty-eight miles they would reach the town of Talsarnau on the coast of North Wales. It had been dull and showery when they started out on Saturday morning laden with tents and sleeping bags, but by the time they were making camp in a field near Welshampton the weather was clearing, and their tramp on the next day had been mostly in sunshine. They had found their way by lanes and tracks over the rounded border hills, and in the late afternoon had come down a side glen into the deep valley carved by the River Ceiriog, where woods of oak and birch and ash hung in a glory of flaming colors along the craggy hillsides.

They had been lucky — Ann thought so, at least — to find an old stone bridge crossing the river just where John's penciled "beeline" crossed it on the map. They couldn't, of course, stick with absolute exactness to the beeline; that would have meant walking through people's gardens in the first part of the tramp. John's rule was that they must not leave the straight line unless it was absolutely necessary, and must regain it as soon as possible after leaving it. He was strict about this. At noon he had insisted on wading across a stream east of a small village — which meant taking off slacks, boots, and two pairs of socks — although there was a bridge a hundred yards downstream. So Ann enjoyed plodding dryshod across the Ceiriog bridge although she was tired and the heavy knapsack had rubbed sore places on her shoulders. A secondary road ran along the flank of the opposite hillside. Climbing to this by a steep lane, and crossing it, they had reached a farmhouse and asked if they might camp on the hill above it. The farmer and his wife had exchanged a word or two in Welsh before giving their consent — a pleasing sign that the beeliners had really crossed into another country — and not only supplied them with two pints of milk but also suggested a good site for their tents. The result was the "really choice" spot where they were now encamped.

A grass track ran up the hillside behind the farm. About two hundred paces along it and just above its level the steep angle of the hill eased in a narrow shelf of grass and bracken with a few trees on it. It sloped only a little and there was just room for Ann's lightweight single-pole tent and John's tiny shelter designed and made by himself. John was proud of this tent. It was nylon with a sewn-in groundsheet and there was just room for him to lie in his sleeping bag. The plan was to use Ann's larger tent for cooking on the solid-fuel stove if it rained but to cook on wood fires, like real tramps, when there was dry fuel. This time they had made a fire from the old branches that lay in the bracken, and had feasted on baked beans and hot cocoa while the sunset colors faded from the darkening sky. Below their hillside ledge there was a ten-foot bank dropping to the track; then a steep slope of two hundred feet to the road with its hedges and telegraph poles; and below the road another drop to the Ceiriog River twisting through the trees in the valley bottom.

"It'd be a bit exposed here if rain blew up from the southwest," John remarked, folding up his map. "But it won't — not tonight, anyhow." He yawned. "We'd better turn in pretty soon. Big day tomorrow. We charge straight over the Berwyn Mountains."

"At Cader Bronwen." Ann nodded.

"That's it. Two thousand five hundred and some odd, and the beeline goes right over the summit. Camp Three will be somewhere in the head of the valley the other side. Let's see. . . ."

"Don't count your chickens," Ann warned.

"*Da iawn*," agreed John, using the Welsh words for "very well."

Because he and his sister were both dark and rather stocky, and had an "e" in their surname, John had a theory that they were descended from some Welsh raider — it was a Welsh prince in his more romantic moments — who had invaded the Midlands hundreds of years ago. Ann had her doubts, based on family history. But John lost no chance of being as Welsh as possible when he was in Wales, and had been particularly pleased that the farmer had understood him when he said good night in Welsh.

The sound of a car engine came from the road below their hillside and they saw the moving glow of its headlights on the treetops in the valley. There was a little traffic on the road because the Ceiriog glen was practically a dead end, with only narrow lanes climbing out over high passes. The white headlight glow revealed how dark it had grown.

"Let's have a last blaze-up," John said.

He scooped a handful of dry twigs from

15

the rim of the embers and threw them on the fire, and the leaping flames illuminated the orange fabric of the tent and turned the valley below into a black void. It was like being inside a Japanese lantern swinging in the night, Ann thought, hugging her knees. She was not so romantically minded as her brother, but journeying cross-country and living in the open — much as people had done before there were such things as roads or cars or even houses — struck her now as being the kind of adventure she liked best.

The flames began to sink and the dark shapes of the hills emerged once more from the blackness. John meditatively dropped a last twig on the fire and then rummaged in the bracken for a flat stone to scoop earth over the embers. Another car was coming up the valley, traveling fast. Ann heard the tires squeal as the brakes were fiercely applied. It must have stopped on the road below their farm. In that same moment there came the sound of footsteps approaching up the track — running footsteps, that stumbled as they came. John stopped rummaging and stood up, and as he turned the footsteps stopped at the foot of the bank below their campsite. Someone scrabbled up the bank and fell on hands and knees two paces from the dying fire. It was a girl.

The little flame from John's last twig showed her untidy fair hair and thin, pale face. She was wearing a jacket and trousers and had a knapsack on her back, and when she managed to speak through her desperate panting, the words came like sobs.

"Hide me . . . please . . . hide me!"

For a second or two the beeliners were too startled to reply. John found his voice first.

"Who's after you?" he asked quickly.

"Policemen," gasped the girl.

"Why?" Ann shot the question at her, frowning. "What have you done?"

"Nothing . . . it's a mistake . . . I'm not a criminal or anything — "

She stopped dead, listening. Down by the farm a man's voice shouted, "Up here?" and they heard someone reply. The girl got to her feet and clutched at John's arm.

"I swear — on my honor — I haven't committed a crime," she panted. "Please, please hide me!"

Ann, still frowning, was going to ask more questions, but John acted at once.

"Into the tent — this one," he said, pushing the newcomer in front of him as he spoke. "Lie flat along the wall at the back and keep perfectly still."

The girl crept in past Ann, who was not too eager to let her pass, and did as John told her. All three of them could hear heavy steps coming up the track.

"Ann, get that sleeping bag off and cover her with it. Quick as you can."

"I'm in my pajamas," Ann objected.

"Never mind that — be *quick*!" said her brother. "Now lean your back against it and do something sort of casual — eat a biscuit out of that packet."

The hurrying footsteps — two men, by the sound of them — were very close. John flung another handful of twigs on the fire and squatted down by it, whistling a tune out of Mozart's *"Eine Kleine Nachtmusik"* rather shakily and a bit flat. The footsteps trampled at the foot of the bank and stopped. A flashlight beamed, a gruff voice said, "Wait," and a man clambered up to the hillside shelf just as the girl had done scarcely more than a minute before him. The flame of the burning twigs winked on the silver buttons of his tunic and showed his peaked uniform cap. He stood up and switched on the flashlight he carried, flashing it first at John and then into the tent where Ann lolled against a shapeless bundle and munched a biscuit.

"Sorry to bother you," he said, switching off the light. "Anyone come past your camp just now?"

"No." John stood up, trying not to look

nervous. "But we heard someone running up the track. It can't have been more than a minute ago, so they can't have gone far." That was true enough, he added to himself. "What's the matter? Are you chasing them?"

But the policeman had already turned away and was sliding down to the track again.

"Get on, man!" they heard him growl to his companion. "Straight on up — only a couple of campers here."

Their boots thudded away up the hill and in fifteen seconds were out of earshot. Ann spoke before the sound of the chase had died away.

"Don't you think that was rather silly?" she demanded sharply. "We've told lies to the police, and even if this girl's not a criminal — "

"I told you, I'm *not*!" interrupted a muffled voice. "And I'm suffocating under here — "

"Pipe down, both of you!" snapped John; he was feeling a bit doubtful himself, but excitement drowned his doubt. "I didn't actually tell lies, and anyway we've got to go through with it now."

"No, you haven't." The girl had pushed her way out of the tent and was standing be-

19

side him. "I can dodge back to the road. Thank you both awfully for — "

"There'll be another policeman by the car. You'd never get clear."

"I'll go up the hillside, then." She sounded desperate.

"In the dark? Through thickets and brambles?"

John could see how utterly tired she was, even by the dim glow from the fire. She was about the same age as he was, and not quite as tall.

"Listen," he said rapidly. "When they don't catch up with you they'll come back down the track. It's long odds they'll take another look at our tents — that's what I'd do if I were those policemen, anyway. So we'll hide you outside the tents somewhere until they've had their look. Right?"

"*I* think it'd be better to let her go," Ann objected stubbornly.

"Well, I don't. You get into that sleeping bag and look as if you're snugging up for the night. You" — John caught hold of the fugitive's hand — "come with me. And look out for the guy lines."

Behind the tents, where the slope steepened below the trees, the bracken stood high, though some of the russet-gold fronds were already leaning sideways against their neighbors. It was too dark now to see the dead branch that lay in the bracken, but John knew where it was because he had broken wood for the fire from it. He guided the girl behind the branch and made her lie down there.

"You'll be all right," he said reassuringly. "Get as close to the ground as you can. We'll see you through."

"I don't know why you should," she said wearily as she crawled in beneath the screen of bracken and branches. "You don't know anything about me — you don't even know my name. It's Ilonka Kazinczy, and I'm — "

"Tell us afterward," John said in a hurried whisper. "They're back."

He covered the few yards to the tents as swiftly and silently as he could, and was just in time to be kneeling by the doorway of his one-man tent when the policemen climbed up to the shelf. There were two of them, out of breath and looking rather big and frightening in the darkness. John was sure they had returned quietly in the hope of catching their quarry at the camp, but he did his best to look surprised when the leading policeman's flashlight went on and shone steadily on him.

"We're back, as you see." It was the policeman who had spoken to him before;

he sounded friendly enough. "Just wanted to ask if you saw anything of the person you heard going up the track."

John stood up, blinking at the flashlight. "Not a thing. You can't see the track from here — and it's dark anyway. You didn't catch her, then?" he added.

The instant he had said it he realized his mistake, with a shock that sent a cold thrill of fear up his spine. The police officer pounced on it at once.

"How d'you know it was a girl if you didn't see her?" he said accusingly.

John stood tongue-tied, but Ann came to his rescue. She had wriggled to the door of the tent in her sleeping bag.

"We thought it was a girl or a woman, officer," she said. "We heard her voice."

"Oh?" To John's relief the flashlight was turned on Ann. "She spoke to you?"

"No — she was sort of talking to herself. And panting at the same time."

John suddenly remembered the odd name the girl had told him. "It seemed to be in a foreign language," he put in. "So we couldn't understand a word."

"Likely enough," muttered the second policeman.

"Um." The man with the flashlight swept the beam across the tents and back again.

"Nice little setup you've got here. Mind if I take a look? — Excuse me, miss."

He shone the light past Ann into the farthest corners of her tent, then stepped to the smaller tent beside it and did the same for that. Finally he sent the circle of light stabbing up to the bracken slope below the trees and moved it slowly across, while John held his breath. Nothing showed or stirred up there and at last the flashlight was switched off.

"Well, I'm sorry to have disturbed you, as I said before," said the policeman slowly. "On a camping holiday, are you?"

"Yes," John answered, hoping his sigh of relief hadn't been noticed.

"Camping here for long?"

"No — we're moving on tomorrow."

"Across the Berwyns?"

"That's it," said John without thinking.

"Ah. Our young lady might be intending to do that, too. If you come across her, ring the police, will you? She's described as about fifteen, height five-four, blonde, dark jacket and trousers, carrying knapsack. Just ask the operator for Police — you won't have to pay. Well — good night to you."

He was turning away when Ann stopped him with a question.

"But what do the police want her for, officer?"

"Questioning, miss," said the policeman. "Seems she did a bunk from London, where she's badly wanted. General call went out this morning. She was spotted at Gobowen, traced to Glyn Ceiriog, seen heading up the road this way. We had her in the headlights as we came around the bend and saw her dodge up by the farm. And then," he ended ruefully, "we lost her after all. No use beating the thickets for her in the dark."

"What'll you do now?" Ann asked.

"Oh, we'll get her all right, don't you worry, miss. Twenty-four hours, forty-eight at most. She's got to come down to a road sometime, if only for food. All the hill farms will be warned, patrol cars on the move — you can't dodge the police for long these days, you know." He touched his cap, silhouetted against the brightening stars. "If you see her you know what to do. Sweet dreams, both of you."

The two policemen scrambled down the bank and were gone. Not until their heavy footsteps had passed far down the track did John let out his breath in a great *Whoosh!* He was trembling all over, he discovered.

"By golly, that was mighty close!" he said; his voice was shaky, too. "Your bit about hearing her voice was pretty average good, Ann."

"I had to get you out of *your* jam," Ann said rather sharply. "But goodness knows what we do now. How on earth shall we — "

John didn't stay to listen. He was already pushing through the bracken behind the tents, toward the big dead branch. The girl was still lying flat on her face under the branch, and when he bent to touch her he could feel that she was sobbing violently.

"It's all right," he said awkwardly. "They've gone — there's the car going now. Hear it?"

The drone of the police car dwindled away into the distance. The girl sat up and seemed to be rubbing her hands across her face.

"I'm s-sorry," she gulped. "I just had to have a cry — it's because I'm so tired, I think."

She was certainly tired, so tired she could hardly stand. John had to put his arm around her to help her to the front of the tents.

"She's about all in," he said to Ann, who was huddled in her sleeping bag in the tent doorway. "Move over and let's get her inside."

Ann moved over, not very willingly, and the girl collapsed limply against her as John took his arm away. He crawled in on her other side and propped her up between them.

"In my opinion," he told his sister, "we ought to let her lie down and sleep. There's room in your tent and she can have my sleeping bag. She can tell us in the morning what it's all about."

"No," Ann said very firmly. "I shan't sleep a wink until I know what you've let us in for. We've told lies to the police — both of us have — and it's up to her to — "

"You're perfectly right."

The girl who called herself Ilonka Kazinczy spoke quite as firmly as Ann. She was sitting up very straight now and pushing the hair from her face, which showed as a pale blur in the darkness.

"I must have some sleep," she went on, "but I'll tell you my story first. I owe you that, at least."

# A Change of Plan

OUTSIDE the tent it was quite dark now. The Ceiriog valley was a pit of blackness and the hills above it seemed pasted against the starry sky like shapes cut out of black cardboard. A little chill wind stirred the bracken fronds and set the embers of the fire glowing like rubies, and the three in the tent drew farther back so that Ann could tuck in the bottom of the door curtain and keep their feet warm.

Ilonka Kazinczy seemed in no hurry to tell John and Ann the story she had promised them. In the brief silence they could hear the murmur of the river far below, now louder, now softer as the little wind played with

the sound. Ann broke the silence, impatiently.

"Well?" she prompted. "You're badly
wanted by the police in London — is that
right?"

John felt Ilonka give a start, as if she had
been lost in thought.

"I'm sorry," she said. "I was trying to
think where to begin, and my mind isn't
working very well. Yes — I suppose it's
right. But it's my uncle Zoltan who's set the
police looking for me. At least, I expect he
has."

"Why?" Ann demanded.

Ilonka wriggled her shoulders. "Let me
begin at the beginning, please. First of all,
I'm Hungarian, as you've probably guessed
from my name, Ilonka Margit Kazinczy. I
don't know your names, by the way."

"I'm John Davies," John said, "and Ann's
my sister. We've got a week's holiday and
we're walking a beeline to the sea, camping
on the way. You don't sound Hungarian,"
he added.

"Well, I've been at school in London since
I was five," she explained, "so I speak English and Hungarian equally well. We came
to England two years before that — my
parents and I. We were refugees. There'd
been a revolution, and terrible fighting. You

28

probably don't know about it at all — most English people don't."

"I do, a bit," John declared; he had been doing Modern History at school. "The Communists took over, didn't they? The Soviets, and all that."

"You're just as bad as the rest of the English," Ilonka said wearily. "The Communists — which means Russia — had enslaved Hungary by nineteen hundred forty-nine. The revolution was in October nineteen fifty-six, when the true Hungarians rose to try and free our country. My father was a true Hungarian. The revolution failed and thousands of people were killed, but we managed to escape with our lives. They say two hundred thousand Hungarians got away safely and went to live in other countries."

She was silent for a moment, staring at the glow of the dying embers. Starlight and firelight between them showed her face in the darkness, the intent face of a young enchantress weaving a spell. This was Ann's impression when she glanced sideways at the older girl, wondering what it was like to leave your home forever and spend all your life in a foreign country. Ann didn't want to feel sympathetic. She resented Ilonka's breaking into the quiet holiday adventure she and her brother had planned. So she hardened her heart and spoke sharply.

"What's this got to do with your uncle, and you being chased by the police?"

"I'm coming to that," Ilonka said. "A year ago — I was just fourteen — my mother and father were killed in a train accident."

"Awful for you," John muttered.

"I went to live with my uncle Zoltan — Zoltan Melich, Mother's brother. He'd left Hungary soon after we did, and was living in London, but we hadn't seen much of him because Father didn't like him. I didn't like him either." Ilonka shivered. "He lived alone, with a housekeeper, and they were both beastly to me — just *beastly*. I went on going to the same school and had friends there, but I hadn't got a home anymore. I had to stay with Uncle Zoltan because he was my guardian. At last things got so bad I couldn't stand it anymore. I decided to run away."

"Good for you," John said. "But where could you run to?"

Ilonka hesitated. "Well — there was only one place I could think of. My father had a brother, a Hungarian refugee like himself. I'd only seen Uncle Gyula once or twice when I was little. He's an artist, and lives by himself in a cottage in North Wales, not far from the coast. I thought if I could get to him, and refuse to leave him, he might arrange to be my guardian instead of Uncle Zoltan. So last night I got out of the house without anyone knowing. I had a few things in a knapsack, and all the money I'd got, which wasn't much — "

"Did you telephone your Uncle Gy — Gyula to tell him you were coming?" interrupted Ann.

"I couldn't. His cottage is in a mountain valley and isn't on the phone."

"You could have written, though."

Ilonka sighed and her body sagged against Ann's. She was trembling as though with cold, and Ann couldn't help putting a comforting arm round her.

"I'm too tired to explain properly," Ilonka murmured. "There wasn't time to write — I decided to run away all in one evening. I caught a train from Euston and got off at a place called Gobowen. I didn't know Wales at all, but I thought I could walk and get lifts until I reached Uncle Gyula's cottage."

"Where is it, exactly?" inquired John.

"I only know it's near a very small village called Croesor, about seven miles from the coast of Caernarvonshire." Her voice was getting sleepier and sleepier. "I got on a bus, and then had a lift from a grocer's truck, and then I was walking miles up this

31

valley and it was getting dark. A car was coming and it had a blue light on the roof. I thought the police might be after me so I started to run up this track — and that's all."

"But — surely you didn't expect your uncle would start the police chasing you, just because you'd left his house," Ann said incredulously.

"You don't know my uncle Zoltan. I do."

The Hungarian girl seemed to be making an effort to speak clearly. Her words tended to run into each other.

"He's my guardian — until I'm twenty-one. When I'm twenty-one I come into a lot of money, because Father was quite rich. Uncle Zoltan hates to let me out of his sight, even. And he knows plenty of high-ups, people who'd help him to . . . to . . ."

Her voice trailed off into a mumble and her head sank against Ann's shoulder. John, who had been frowning over the brief details of Ilonka's journey, spoke suddenly.

"When did you eat last, Ilonka?"

She roused herself to reply. "I had a cup of tea and some cake — that was eleven this morning, at Euston."

"Good grief!" exclaimed John, getting up in a hurry. "No wonder you're all in. Supper — that's what you want."

"Please — I just couldn't eat a thing," Ilonka protested.

"All right then — hot milk and sugar. I'll get it now. Won't take a minute."

John dived into his coffinlike tent to get his sleeping bag, which he tossed into Ann's lap.

"Get her into that," he told his sister. "I'll brew some hot milk and then she can sleep in your tent."

Ilonka began to object that she couldn't take his sleeping bag, but he cut her short by vanishing into the darkness to gather dry twigs.

The ashes of the fire still had a red glow in them and the little pyramid of twigs soon blazed up under John's scientific puffing. He put a mugful of milk into the pan and balanced it carefully on two flat stones over the fire. Then he dived into his tent again and came out with a map and the pencil-type flashlight he carried for use in emergencies such as the tents blowing down in the night. On the map, which was Sheet 116 of the One-Inch Ordnance Survey, he searched for the village of Croesor. It took him some time to find it because he had to keep one eye on the milk, but he spotted it at last, a tiny place at the seaward end of a glen running down from the Moelwyn Range. The mountains

cut it off completely on the east, and the
only way to it from that side was over a
high pass, where the map marked a path.
Talsarnau, the place on the coast where the
proposed beeline ended, was only six miles
south of it.

Frowning thoughtfully, John switched off
the flashlight and removed the pan from the
fire just as the milk was beginning to bubble.
He filled Ann's mug, stirred in a generous
two spoonfuls of sugar, and took it to the
larger tent. Ilonka was already in his sleeping bag, sitting hunched against Ann and
half asleep. She took the mug with a murmured word of thanks and sipped the milk
eagerly. The arm holding the mug, John noticed, was clad in a pajama sleeve that wasn't
Ann's, so she had not started on her mad
journey without some sort of preparation.
He wondered what else she had packed into
that small knapsack to help her on a journey
across North Wales. A twig flared up briefly
on the embers and lit her face in its frame
of tangled pale-gold hair; the haggard, worried look had gone from it now. She was a
very pretty girl, he decided.

"She can lie along the back wall and use
her clothes for a pillow," Ann said, speaking
across Ilonka as if she weren't there. "What

about you? You'll be cold without a sleeping bag."

"I'll be fine," said John hastily. "With your jacket and Ilonka's and mine as well, I'll be snug as a bug. Feeling a bit better?" he added, taking the empty mug Ilonka held out to him.

She nodded slowly, as if her head were too heavy to hold up. "Much better. Only utterly, frightfully tired. I don't know how to . . . to thank you for . . . "

Her voice broke and she looked as if she were going to cry again. John cut in firmly.

"Just forget it and go to sleep. Don't worry about the future — we're going to see you through. Tuck her in, Ann, will you? I'll be back in a minute."

In fact, his various jobs took him nearly five minutes. He washed out the mug with some water from the folding plastic bucket and stowed it with their other utensils under the eaves of the tent. Then he got some earth and sprinkled it over the ashes of the fire, so that if the wind sprang up in the night there would be no blown sparks that might set the bracken alight. When the last faint ruby glow had gone, valley and hillside looked blacker than ever under the canopy of stars. John rummaged in his tent, and with the aid of the pencil flashlight found his Log Book. He always kept a detailed Log of his camping trips, using a notebook and ornamenting his record with little picture maps that gave a rough idea of the sort of country they would be crossing. His Beeline Log was already decorated with three such maps, covering the whole of the journey. Later he was to mark on them a dotted line showing the route they actually took. The picture maps would do for a bit of rough planning. Taking the Log and the flashlight, he returned to Ann's tent.

Ann was still sitting bunched up in her sleeping bag at the doorway, but now she was alone. John squatted beside her.

"Asleep?" he whispered, jerking his head at the dark interior of the tent.

"You needn't whisper," Ann said in her ordinary voice. "She dropped off the moment she lay down. She's sleeping like a log. I don't know whether *I* shall," she added. "Ilonka snores. You can hear her."

Snoring didn't fit in with John's romantic idea of the situation.

"In my opinion," he said rather stiffly, after listening, "that's just deep breathing. Anyway, let's keep our voices down. We've got to do some planning. What was in her knapsack besides pajamas — did you see?"

"I felt," corrected his sister, "when I was getting her pajamas out for her. It was too dark to see. There was a wool sweater, a toothbrush, and a comb, and a parcel wrapped in paper, quite small."

"No map or compass?"

"I'm pretty certain there wasn't."

John whistled. "Not much of an outfit for crossing the Welsh mountains. Did she talk at all while I wasn't there?"

"Not much. I asked her if she'd ever been in Wales before and she said No, only to Scotland for a ski course last winter. She put on her ski outfit for this running-away trip." Ann groped behind her and held up a boot. "Her boots are ski boots, so she's probably telling the truth about that."

"Smooth under toe and heel," observed John, running his hand over the boot before setting it down, "but we're not doing any rock climbing, so it doesn't matter all that much. I wonder how she expected to find this Croesor place without a map. She was mighty lucky to find us, you know."

Ann said nothing for a second or two and then spoke in an odd voice.

"John — you don't believe that tale she told us, do you?"

John stared at the dark shape of his sister. "Why? Don't you?"

"I don't believe the police would be chasing her like this just because she left her uncle's house. It was only last night she left. Surely anyone — even Uncle Zoltan or whatever his name is — would wait to see if she turned up next day before they made such a fuss."

"She did explain that," John pointed out. "If Zoltan's such a nasty piece of work as she — "

"And another thing," Ann interrupted, hurrying on. "Suppose she managed to get to this other uncle, the artist, what could he do? If Zoltan's her proper guardian, wouldn't the law send her back to him right away?"

"I don't know," John said slowly. "But perhaps she didn't stop to think of that. She's been badly scared — you can tell that."

"Yes. Scared of something more than just Uncle Zoltan and being brought back by the police."

John shifted his position impatiently.

"Now look," he said. "She told us on her honor she hadn't committed a crime. Does she look like a criminal to you?"

"No-o," Ann said slowly. "She seems quite

a nice sort of girl. I only think she hasn't been honest with us. And," she added, being honest herself, "I'm not too keen on taking her across North Wales. That's what's in your mind, isn't it?"

"Yes," said John with a touch of defiance. "What else d'you suggest? Phone a police station, like that policeman told us? Turn her out tomorrow to be caught?"

Ann was silent. He reached over to lay a hand on her knee.

"Look, Ann," he said persuasively, "we can't do anything else. We've made ourselves sort of responsible for Ilonka, and we've just got to see it through. It was a terrific stroke of luck for her, finding us — the only people for miles around who'd be able to help her. We can get her to Croesor all right, steering by the hill tracks and keeping clear of roads —"

"It means giving up the beeline," Ann said in a flat voice.

"Yes — but this'll be much more of an adventure. Real John Buchan stuff." John knew his sister liked reading the old Buchan spy stories. "Escape over the hills, dodging the police, and all that — and the police won't have a search party on the Welsh mountains just for a runaway niece. Even if we got found out, it wouldn't be serious. We couldn't be fined or imprisoned for helping a girl to get from one uncle to another. Well — what d'you say?"

Ann said nothing for a moment, and still sounded doubtful when she spoke.

"I think Ilonka's got a secret she hasn't told us. But I suppose you're right, and we're bound to help her. What's the plan?"

John gave her knee a squeeze. "Nice work. You're a pretty average good partner, Ann. Now" — the pencil flashlight flicked on, spotlighting the Log open on the tent floor between them — "I'll have to work out a detailed route with the big maps in the morning, but these sketch maps will do for a start. Here's the rough idea."

Afterward, Ann always thought of this moment as the real beginning of their adventures — the stars shivering in the vast dark dome of the sky, the hills like giant black beasts crouched motionless opposite the tent, the chill of the night air on her cheek, the heavy breathing of the runaway girl just behind her, and John's voice, low but excited, methodically outlining the new route of their journey.

"General direction's still west, but we'll have to go a bit north of the beeline route and do more zigzagging. Not far north, though, because the A5 runs east-west all along there and we must keep clear of it. Can't cross the Berwyns over Cader Bronwen tomorrow — that was going to take us through Bala, quite a town and right on the beeline. We'll have to cross farther north and then find a bridge over the River Dee. After that there's a rare tangle of hills and valleys, and some minor roads to cross — worse luck! — until we get to about *here*, east of Blaenau Festiniog. It could be tricky dodging that place. Roads and slate quarries and so on. But we ought to find a way around and up to the pass over the Moelwyns. That'll bring us straight down to Croesor."

"And then?" prompted Ann as he stopped.

"Why, then we deliver Ilonka to her uncle and push on to Talsarnau and the coast," said John, switching off the light and putting the Log in his pocket. "I'll make Ilonka promise not to tell anyone about us and that'll be the end of it."

In spite of her doubts Ann found herself getting interested in the new plan. Resentment at Ilonka's intrusion was giving way to a feeling that this might be fun.

"It sounds all right," she said. "But what about food?"

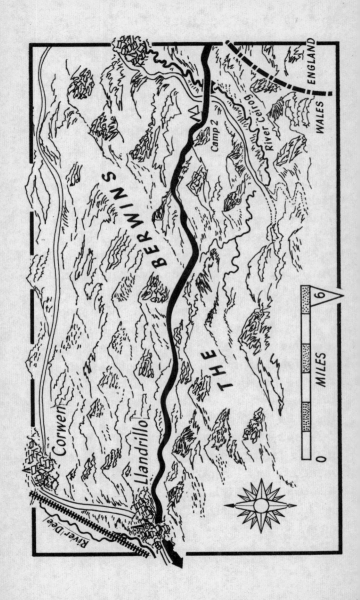

"Easy. Our camps — we should manage with only three — will have to be well hidden, not too far from a village with a shop. I can run down and buy what we want."

"Before closing time," Ann warned. "Which means pitching camp early. And if Ilonka's going to use your sleeping bag you'll be without one."

"I can take it." John peered at the luminous dial of his watch. "Good grief! It's after eleven already. Hand out those two jackets and I'll turn in. We don't know whether Ilonka's any good at hill walking, so we'll make an early start tomorrow."

Ann gave him the jackets, and with a whispered *"Nos da!"* he wriggled feet first into his tiny tent.

John knew from camping experience that sleeping in your clothes is a bad thing and colder than you expect. He got into pajamas, with some difficulty in the confined space and pitch darkness, and arranged his clothes over hips and shoulders where he usually felt the cold most. Under him was Ann's jacket with his spare sweater on it, insulating his upper half from the chilly groundsheet; he put a spare pair of socks on his feet and put his feet into his empty knapsack, wrapping his own jacket around knees and thighs.

Ilonka's jacket he reserved for putting around his shoulders.

The exertion of getting himself snug had made him almost hot, and he felt warm enough and tired enough to go to sleep at once; but the excitement of the evening kept him awake for a while, with his thoughts centered on Ilonka Kazinczy. Her story *was* a bit strange, come to think of it. Ann had some excuse for thinking so, at any rate. But a girl like Ilonka couldn't have done anything really wrong, even if she hadn't told them the whole truth about herself. He'd see she got safely to her uncle at Croesor. Finding a route across mountain country, clear of roads and houses, was a job right up John Davies' street — he was quite confident of that. Tomorrow they'd go straight up the hillside from the campsite instead of following the track. There was a pass a bit north of Cader Bronwen. . . .

He snuggled Ilonka's jacket around his ears and tried to project a picture of the One-Inch map on the darkness. But before he could do that he was asleep.

# Getaway

JOHN woke with a start, in his mind a vague recollection of having wakened several times before and feeling cold. It wasn't the cold that worried him now, though. In the instant of waking a thought had blazed up as if it had been smoldering in him all night; a most unpleasant thought. *Surely the police, knowing that Ilonka had gone up the hillside track, would leave someone on watch!*

He sat up, throwing off his covering of clothes and jackets, and looked at his watch. Half past eight — and he had intended to get away early! Why was the tent so dark if it was that late? He untied the door fastenings and stuck out his head, to find there was nothing at all to be seen except a blank wall of grayish-white fog, a morning mist that had flooded the deep Ceiriog valley and risen to engulf the little tents on the hillside above. It was a cold and clammy mist, and though its chill had awakened him earlier, its effect of lingering darkness had made him turn over and go to sleep again. There was no sound of movement from the other tent, and with this new fear in his mind John wasn't going to rouse them yet. He put on his clothes and boots, took the pan and the empty plastic bucket from outside the tent, and got down the bank to the track without making any noise. The white mist was like a blanket moving away in front of him as he walked quickly down to the farm gate at the bottom.

The farm dogs were not the barking sort, and there was only a brief growl from inside the farmhouse when John knocked on the door. The farmer's wife opened the door. When she saw who it was she smiled and asked if it was milk he wanted.

"A pint of milk, please," John said, "and perhaps I could have some water in this bucket. And" — he stopped and gulped — "and two eggs, if you can spare them."

He had been going to say "three eggs." Just in time he had seen who was sitting at the table in the farm kitchen, with his tunic unbuttoned. It was a policeman.

"Morning," said the policeman, leaning sideways to get a look at him.

John forced himself to grin. "Good morning. Found that girl you were after last night?"

It was the constable who had been with the senior police officer when the tents were searched. He grinned back at John and sipped his tea.

"We'll get her today," he said. "Ten o'clock, there'll be a dozen men starting up the hills from this side, at various points. She won't have got far in the night, if she's moved at all."

"That's exciting!" said the farmer's wife, coming back with the milk, water, and eggs. "But I'm sorry for the poor child, whatever she's done. I hope you don't catch her, Tom Lewis — and there's for you!"

The constable started to reply but John wasn't listening. He paid for the eggs and milk, thanked the farmer's wife for letting them camp, and got back to the tents as fast as he could. They were still wrapped in thick mist, but he saw that the door of Ann's tent was half open and that they were moving about inside.

"We've got to bundle and go right away," he said, quietly so as not to frighten Ilonka. "Ann, strike tent and pack up soon as possible — breakfast comes later."

Ann's head poked out of the tent. Her dark hair was tousled and her brown eyes wide with alarm.

"Why?" she asked.

"They're starting to search the hillsides at ten. There's a policeman at the farm now." John gulped some milk and placed the bottle by the tent. "Finish this between you — it's all we'll have until we're a long way from here. Hurry!"

Ann asked no more questions, but he could hear her answering Ilonka's anxious inquiries as he got to work taking down his tent and stowing things in his knapsack. He felt too angry with himself to be scared. What an idiot he'd been not to think of the obvious precaution the police would take! (The eggs could go in the pot, packed with his spare undershirt.) If that constable had been a bit smarter at his job, and strolled up the track while the three of them were talking, Ilonka would be in the bag by now. (Half a loaf, cheese, chocolate — enough for lunch, anyway.) Come to think of it, the constable might walk up the track at any moment for an after-breakfast stroll. The sooner they got away, the better. Thank goodness for the mist — but it was only morning mist and wouldn't last long. He spared a moment for a glance at Sheet 117 of the One-Inch map, put it in his pocket with his compass, and hurried over to help the girls with their tent.

Ilonka greeted him with a rather nervous smile.

"Seems I've let you in for trouble straight away," she said. "I really think you'd better let me try to get through by myself."

"You'd never make it, in my opinion," John said gruffly. "If you can squeeze Ann's sleeping bag into your sack, it'll help."

Ilonka did as he suggested without further protest. She was just as pretty by the foggy morning light as by firelight, he noticed. She had combed her fair hair back and tied it with a scrap of ribbon, and was looking fresh and alert although there had been no time for a wash. He remembered the plastic bucket full of water, and when packing up was finished, they all had what John called "a quick rinse" before starting up the hillside.

"No talking from now on," John ordered

as he led off, "and as little noise as possible."

The morning's events had made him resolve to be more careful. Some farmhand coming down the track might hear them on the hillside and tell the farmer; the farmer would know then that they hadn't gone up the track toward Cader Bronwen, as John had told him they would. Little things like that could easily set the police on Ilonka's track — which was his and Ann's track now. John was beginning to realize what a responsibility he had accepted.

The fog clung around them as they climbed straight up the angle of the hill. It was a typical Berwyn hillside, steep as a precipice but clothed with grass and dying bracken, scrub oak, and brambles. In ten minutes it was plain that Ilonka was slower on such ground than John and his sister. She hesitated and slipped instead of stepping up confidently, puffed and panted, had to be waited for. John, halting to wait for the second time, seethed with impatience until he remembered that Ilonka hadn't eaten anything since yesterday morning. Obviously she would have to get some food inside her at the first opportunity; but that could only be when they were safe from pursuit.

The angle of the ground eased and there

were fewer bushes and trees. A wire fence loomed out of the thick mist on the hill brow, and when they had climbed over this they found themselves treading heather. John halted to use his compass and allow Ilonka to get her breath. He had been heading west-northwest up the hill. From here, as he had noted on the map, a course almost due west for two miles ought to bring them to a track running along the ridge — an ancient track, for it was marked "Ffordd Saeson," the Saxons' Road. Nine fifty by his watch. In ten minutes the searchers would be climbing up from the Ceiriog valley. Compass in hand, he set out at a steady pace up the heathery slope, with the girls close behind him.

Though the route was still uphill, the angle was much gentler. Ann, who knew that it is always discouraging to be last in a line of hill walkers, had made Ilonka go in front of her and the Hungarian girl was keeping up well. It was hard going, all the same, with the wet heather stalks whipping their ankles and nothing to see but the everlasting white wall of mist ahead. They walked without speaking, saving their breath for speed. Suddenly John gave a grunt of satisfaction — they had found the path. The Saxons' Road was no more than a sheep track now, but it took them along more quickly and soon began to descend across a hillside of tall heather with an invisible stream rumbling in the mist below. Rifts opened in the white vapor, revealing patches of forestry close below them, with a broad track climbing through the young larches. The ground flattened out beside a curious mound of stones and heather. The mist fled away as if by magic, and with startling suddenness a vast empty landscape opened in front of them.

"The Berwyns, John!" exclaimed Ann excitedly. "Oh, this is really choice!"

And there it was, the long purple-brown ridge of the Berwyns, rolling far away against a pale-blue sky flecked with white clouds. Between the low pass where they were standing and the hills they had to cross stretched a trackless wilderness of gold and green, sprawling moorland and marshy glen. John, with an uneasy glance at the forestry track that climbed from the mist-filled valley behind them, got out his map.

"Bang on," he said after a moment. "There's the Mound of the Pass. Sou'-sou'-west across this marshy bit, around the corner of that hill over there, and we'll strike the track that crosses the Berwyns. The pass is just under two thousand."

"Can't we stop for some food?" Ann said. "Ilonka must need it badly."

"I *am* rather hungry," Ilonka said hesitantly.

John shook his head and peered at the map. "We'll eat in about forty minutes. Fast as we can go until then."

Once again they were marching at full speed. Down a boggy slope, across the headwaters of a reedy stream, up the stony turf of the hillside beyond. Behind and on their left the mist still lay in swathes over the heathery ridge they had just crossed, and all three fugitives began to cast uneasy glances over their shoulders at those dark slopes. It was very plain that they would be in full view of any pursuers who emerged from the mist. John was thinking how unsuitably they were dressed for hiding in the hills — he and Ann in bright-blue jackets, Ilonka in her navy-blue ski suit. But it was impossible not to feel cheerful with the keen mountain air on their faces, and the bare hillside bright with autumn sunshine, and small blue cloud shadows sliding across the russet moors. Ann hummed a tune and John started to whistle a bit of *"Eine Kleine Nachtmusik."* This was when they rounded a corner of the hill and came in sight of a narrow valley down on the left, with a green track coming up it. There were sheepfolds beside the track but no farms in sight. Scrubby gorse grew on the slopes here, and — following John's example — the girls collected the dry sticks from under the bushes as they passed.

John halted at last, in a fold or groove of the hillside with a tiny stream tumbling down it to join the bigger stream in the valley.

"Knapsacks off!" he announced. "They can't possibly spot us here."

"Touch wood," remarked Ann, brandishing her armful of gorse sticks.

Ilonka sank down with a sigh on a flat ledge of turf beside the stream. "At this moment," she declared more than half seriously, "I couldn't cross a two-thousand-foot pass to save my life."

"You will, though, in half an hour," said John.

He had found two big flat stones and was carefully building a pyramid of gorse sticks between them, little twigs at first and bigger ones as the pyramid grew. A bit of paper at the bottom blazed as John lit it with a match, and the twigs caught and held the flame just as Ann came up with the pan containing two inches of water from the stream. The gorse burned hotly and quickly. It took all the wood they had collected to keep the two eggs boiling for five minutes, but that was all they needed.

"Boiled eggs, two for Ilonka," said John, placing them on the turf beside her. "Likewise brown bread and butter. To follow, cheese or chocolate. Tonight we'll dine a bit more sumptuously."

Ilonka wanted to share the eggs equally among the three of them but gave up the idea when Ann pointed out that it meant dividing both eggs into three parts. She ate eagerly, while John and Ann finished the last of the loaf with some wrapped cheese and two bars of chocolate. It was a moot point, John remarked, whether this was breakfast or lunch, the time being exactly noon. Ilonka, with her mouth full, suggested they could call it "brunch." All things considered, it was a surprisingly cheerful meal.

Indeed, it was hard to believe there were such things as policemen and angry uncles, up here in the empty hills where nothing moved except the little stream and the white specks of sheep on the distant slopes. The green track below them looked as if no one had walked up it for a hundred years. It was an old drove track, said John, and if it was used at all it was only by hill shepherds moving their sheep across the high Berwyn barrier. Ilonka bent over the map he had spread on his knee.

"I'm not much good at maps," she said. "Is this a road where your finger is?"

"Yes. We get down to that from the Berwyns. It runs from Corwen to Bala up the valley of the River Dee — this wiggly blue line." John moved his finger on the map. "That river's a bit of a problem. It's a biggish river, the sort you've got to cross by a bridge. This track below us ends by coming down to Llandrillo, where there's a bridge over the Dee, but we must avoid going through Llandrillo if we can — it's a large village and there's probably a police station there."

"Oh! What do we do, then?"

"See this black-and-white line? That's a railway, but it's not used now. *That* crosses the Dee by a bridge, a mile from Llandrillo. If we get on the railway line and walk along it to the bridge, we can get to these lanes on the far side of the valley and dodge up into the hills to make camp."

Ann had come to look over his shoulder. "If we left the lane above Llandrillo," she said, "and cut straight down, we could pop across the road and get on the railway track without coming near the village."

"That's it," John agreed, folding up the map. "The other problem is how to get hold of some food. I think I'd better go into Llandrillo by myself and buy some. That'll be safe enough."

"I think it's absolutely marvelous the way you work everything out," Ilonka said. "But" — she hesitated — "are you really sure the police aren't catching up on us while we're stopping here?"

She spoke lightly, but Ann saw the strained look on her face and the anxiety that shone in her hazel-green eyes.

"Don't see how they can be." John, who had reddened at Ilonka's praise, spoke confidently. "We were out of sight up this valley before they came out of the mist on that hilltop, and it's very unlikely they'd guess we've taken this route. When they've finished beating the hillside where you were last seen and haven't found you, they'll turn in and concentrate on watching the roads."

"Or even give up altogether," Ann said, watching Ilonka. "After all, they can't possibly use a lot of policemen all day long just for chasing Uncle Zoltan's missing niece."

Ilonka darted a glance at her and looked

away quickly. "Let's hope you're right," was all she said.

"In my opinion," John said, "we've made a pretty clean getaway. All the same, we don't want to hang about. There's a longish trek ahead, and we must find a well-hidden campsite before dark, so let's get weaving."

Ten minutes later they were down on the green track and tramping uphill toward the pass over the Berwyns. Behind them the glen came winding up from the hidden lower valleys; ahead the track climbed steeply along the side of a boggy stream. There was not a soul about. John set a slower pace now, but even so Ilonka was plainly tiring when at last the track curled around a knoll of heather into the shallow notch of the pass. She sank down wearily on a big rock at the wayside, and her face showed something of the same desperate, frightened look it had worn when she had first appealed for help. Neither John nor Ann noticed it. They were too engrossed in the enormous view that was spread before them.

The sky had slowly clouded over as they mounted the moorland slopes to the pass, but the far horizon was dark and clear. It was a horizon of mountains. The long rank of peaks stood blue and heart-stirring in the northwest, thirty miles away. From their two-thousand-foot pass the mountainsides swept down to a broad valley where the silver coils of a river gleamed, and between the valley and the far Snowdonian peaks stretched a jumble of hills and mountain ridges shading from brown to purple as they rolled away into the distance.

The shrill "Kee-eerlie!" of a curlew drifting overhead brought Ilonka out of her gloomy thoughts. She got up, rather stiffly, and came to stand beside the others. Her eyes widened in dismay when she saw the wild landscape and the faraway hills.

"Is that where we've got to go?" she asked apprehensively.

"Not toward Snowdon — farther to the west." John pointed to the left of the distant Snowdonian range. "The Arenigs are in the way, so you can't see the Moelwyns. Not so very far, really — two days, and you'll be at your uncle's cottage. It's too cold to stand about here," he added. "Let's get on down."

Up to now the high wall of the Berwyn Mountains, ten miles long, had shielded them from the cool westerly wind, but the chill breath of autumn and coming winter numbed their noses and fingers as they started down the winding track toward the wide valley fifteen hundred feet below. The heather of the crest gave way to bright yellow moorgrass on the hill shoulders lower down, and then to turfy steeps where a few sheep grazed. Ilonka was limping slightly — a sore heel, she told John — and their descent was slow. When they came to a dip in the track, where it crossed a leaping stream by a tumbledown stone bridge, they halted to examine the sore heel and found that a blister had rubbed into a raw place. John covered it with a Band-Aid from his first-aid outfit, and they ate the last of their food — two cubes of chocolate each — before going on.

They saw no one on the path or on the hillsides above and below it, but in twenty minutes they came to a gate and the track headed steeply downhill between stone walls. Patches of woodland appeared not far below, and a farm off to one side of the track. They were nearing the valley and the cold mountain wind had gone. The afternoon was already darkening toward evening when they saw below them a church steeple and a cluster of houses among trees, with the winding Dee half a mile away under the wooded hills of the valley's opposite side.

"Llandrillo," said John, halting and getting out the map. "There's the railway embankment beyond those fields on the other side of the village. We'll go on down here another quarter of a mile and then cut down to cross the road well clear of the houses."

Ilonka drew in her breath sharply, as if she were bracing herself for an ordeal, but she limped resolutely on beside John down the steepening track, which dropped past a copse of ash and fir and suddenly became a well-traveled lane. A farmhouse stood on the hillside a little way below, but they had still seen no one when John stopped again at a bend in the track. It had hazel hedges on each side here, and a stout barbed-wire fence.

"Can't see a gate," said John, "but we'll have to get off the lane now if we're to reach the road without passing close to that farm. Look out for the wire."

He parted the branches of the hedge and began to climb over the barbed wire close to one of the fencing posts. He had got one leg over the top strand when a man's harsh voice spoke from a few yards away and made all three of them jump.

"Caught you at it this time! Breaking my fences!"

He was a small, thin man in a stained

raincoat, with a black-and-white sheepdog at his heels. The rubber boots he was wearing had enabled him to approach silently, coming up the hill and round the bend from the direction of the village. From beneath bushy eyebrows his eyes glared very fiercely at the travelers.

"I — er — er — we thought we'd take a shortcut," John stammered. "We couldn't see a gate, so — "

"I'll find you a shortcut, young man!" snapped the farmer. "I've had three fences damaged by hooligans like you this August, and never caught 'em. Well, I've caught *you*. I was going up for my tea, but *diawl!* I'll deal with you first. You're coming down with me to the police station!"

The words were hardly out of his mouth when there was a sort of stifled shriek from Ilonka. With white face and staring eyes she rushed straight past the farmer and vanished down the lane at top speed.

# Escape to the Woods

For three seconds after Ilonka's mad flight nobody moved. Even the sheepdog had shrunk against his master's legs as she rushed past, and stayed there. Then the farmer turned to stare uneasily at Ann.

"Seems like I scared one of you good and proper, anyway," he said. "White as a sheet, she was."

Ann pounced on this opening. "Of course you scared her!" she said indignantly. "The poor girl's a Hungarian refugee. She thought she'd be taken before the secret police, or the Gestapo, or something."

"That's right." John, who had eased himself unobstrusively out of the hedge, came to her support. "She's a nervous case, sir. My sister and I are looking after her. I think you ought to let us follow her at once — I swear we won't try to get over your fence again."

"If we don't catch her," added Ann, "she might do herself an injury."

"*Diawl!*" muttered the farmer, looking very uneasy indeed. "If I'd known — but go on, go on! Quickly with you! I'll say no more this time!"

John and Ann were racing down the lane before the final words were out of his mouth. When they came around the bend they saw the lane running straight and level past two cottages to emerge in the village less than a quarter of a mile ahead. Four small children were standing in a group close to the hedge on the left, just short of the first cottage. They reached the children, and found that they had gathered to stare at Ilonka, who was slumped dejectedly in the long grass at the roadside nursing her left ankle.

"What happened?" she demanded, gazing anxiously up the lane past John.

"We spun him a yarn and he let us go," John explained between gasps for breath. "Here, you infants," he added, "push off — scram. The lady's quite all right, see?"

"*Are* you all right?" Ann asked as the children, still staring, moved slowly away.

"Why on earth did you have to dash away like that?"

"I panicked, that's all." Ilonka sounded defiant. "If he'd made us go to the police station it would have been the end, wouldn't it? For me, at any rate."

John nodded agreement. "And as it happened it was the best thing you could have done, in my opinion. It was our cue to tell the farmer you're a Hungarian refugee with a thing about secret police. That's why he —"

"*What!* You told him — but don't you see he'll tell his wife, and his wife'll tell the neighbors, and the police will hear about it and know I'm the girl they're after?"

"You'll be in Croesor before that happens," John assured her. "Anything wrong with that ankle you're massaging?"

Ilonka got to her feet and rested her weight gingerly on her left foot. "It seems all right now," she said. "I trod on a loose stone and went flying — on to the grass, luckily."

"That's two bits of luck," John said with a frown. "We need one more — a big bit. We'll have to go right through Llandrillo now."

"Oh, *no!*" Ilonka, her yes wide and frightened, put a hand to her mouth. "I'll be caught — they'll be watching for me."

"Now look, Ilonka," Ann said firmly, "they can't possibly be watching for you everywhere. And anyway, what else can we do? We're practically in Llandrillo now — and those children saw you, besides the farmer."

John laid a hand on the Hungarian girl's arm. He was surprised to feel her trembling.

"We'll make it," he assured her. "If they're on the lookout at all it's for one blonde girl, not three hikers. Ann, you wait here with her. Give me five minutes start, then walk down to the village. I'll meet you on the corner. Ilonka, you'd better hide that hair under your hood."

"Where are you going?" Ann asked as he walked away.

"To buy some food," said John over his shoulder.

He called a cheerful *hiya!* to the four children as he passed them. There were more children playing about near the corner where the lane joined the main road — evidently they had come out of school not long ago — and two elderly women were gossiping outside one of the houses farther up the street. A car passed while he was examining the twisting road through the village for shops and stores, but there seemed to be little traffic and few people about in Llandrillo and certainly no police in sight. There was a small grocer's shop on the opposite side of the road, only a few yards away.

John was back at the corner with a minute to spare. The two girls were coming down the lane, and he had a quick look at the map before they joined him.

"All clear," he announced, stowing the map away. "We go through the village and along the main road three quarters of a mile. Lane on right leads to bridge over Dee. Keep going, steady but not fast. And for goodness' sake, Ilonka, try not to look so scared!"

They began to walk through the quiet village street — quiet, except for the thunder of a farm tractor. A few people were going in and out of the half dozen shops, but no one spared them more than a passing glance. They had almost reached the western limits of Llandrillo when Ilonka clutched at John's arm and hissed a word he couldn't understand.

*"Istenem!"*

"What?" John turned his head. "Oh, yes — there's the village police station. All fast asleep, I shouldn't wonder."

His careless manner wasn't a bit convincing, and to cover Ilonka's obvious fright Ann asked him loudly what he had bought in Llandrillo.

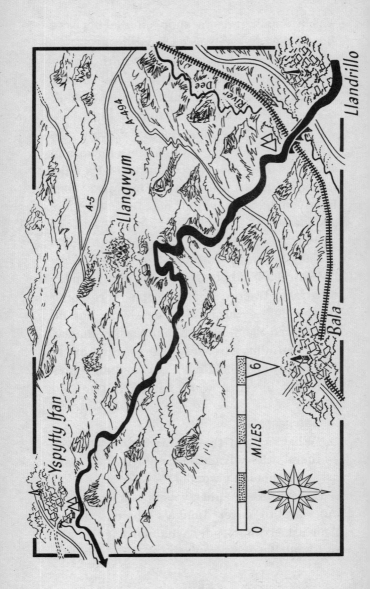

"A lot," answered her brother, wriggling his shoulders under the bulging knapsack. "And don't I know it! Let's see — two loaves, more butter and sugar, half a dozen eggs, cheese, fruit cake, a large can of baked beans for tonight's supper, one can of cocoa. Oh — and six slabs of chocolate."

By this time they were passing the last house of the village. In front the road curved between hedgerows, with the valley fields on the right and a tree-clad hillside rising above on the left. All three of them gave an adible sigh of relief as the village fell behind them; but two cars, whizzing past one after the other, reminded them unpleasantly that there were such things as police patrols.

"Right-hand side of the road, single file," John commanded. "Eyes on the road in front. Ilonka, tuck that bit of hair under your hood. Only half a mile more and we'll be turning off into a lane," he added, noticing her pale and anxious face.

She forced herself to smile. "Good."

They trudged on in silence for five minutes. An ancient truck passed them, and then a bus coming from Bala. It was really extraordinary, thought Ann, how you felt that everyone was looking suspiciously at you when actually they weren't.

"What was that word you said — something like 'issendom'?" she asked Ilonka.

"I expect I said *istenem*. It's what Hungarians say when they're — well, scared stiff, for instance." Ilonka, who was walking in front of Ann, shuddered. "And I *was* scared stiff, passing that police station."

"Funny," Ann said thoughtfully. "I wouldn't have said you were a person who'd scare easily."

"I'm not! But when it's a matter of life and — "

She stopped herself quickly. Ann said nothing aloud, but she reflected that you could hardly call Ilonka's runaway journey "a matter of life and death." More than ever she doubted the Hungarian girl's story.

Only one other vehicle, a baker's truck, passed them before they reached the turning on the right. It was not signposted, and the lane was so narrow and winding that John got out his map again to make sure it led to a bridge over the Dee.

"This is it, all right," he declared after a moment. "Another half hour and we'll be finding a campsite in those woods on the other side of the valley. Not before it's time, either."

October twilight was beginning to filter into the low gray clouds overhead. The yellow leaves had fallen early from the tall hazel hedges that bordered the lane, and a small but chilly wind stirred the branches; moving like witches' fingers against the darkening sky, they looked somehow desolate and threatening. Still, it was good to be turning off the main road, heading toward the wooded hills that stood along the western side of the river valley.

"No police patrol cars'd come this way," John said as they trudged between the hedges. "If there are any, that is. It'd be funny if we've been dodging and skulking for nothing — "

He stopped speaking and looked over his shoulder toward the main road, from which came the sound of a car traveling from the Llandrillo direction. The three had just reached the first bend in the lane, and the next moment John was pushing the girls urgently around it and telling them to crouch down against the bank. He himself stooped so that he could peer through the hedge.

They heard the car pass the end of the lane and go on toward Bala, traveling quite slowly. John straightened up.

"All clear," he said. "Just thought we'd better not take any chances."

"Was it a police car?" Ann asked, brushing dead leaves from her slacks.

"No. Just a small open car — green Morris convertible with the top down. But I happened to see that the passenger was standing up. Seemed to be having a good look at the scenery over the tops of the hedges."

"Or — looking for me," Ilonka said tensely. "Was it a man?"

"Not a policeman, anyway," John reassured her. "Tall chap with a regular mane of gray hair blowing in the wind. The last tourist of summer, probably."

"A mane . . . of gray hair," the girl repeated under her breath, staring at him wide-eyed.

"Yes — policemen have theirs cut pretty short, you know." John settled the heavy knapsack on his shoulders. "Let's press on. The wind's southwest and there could be rain on the way."

They were all feeling tired, and Ilonka was beginning to limp heavily. Five minutes' walking brought them to the bridge, an ancient stone arch crossing the Dee where the river flowed dark and silent between its border fringing of oaks. Just beyond it the lane passed beneath the embankment of the unused railway, and then wound on for another quarter of a mile to a T-junction of even narrower lanes. Once more they seemed to be in a deserted countryside. The trees rose steeply on the hill slopes immediately above; the level valley they had just crossed stretched away behind them to the feet of the Berwyns, whose crinkled flanks were beginning to fade in the gray-blue haze of evening. It was so quiet that the screech of a cock pheasant in the woods overhead made them jump.

John turned left unhesitatingly at the junction. There was not a house in sight, but the muddy lane had tractor marks on it as if it led to a farm, so when they reached a rough track coming down on the right, he left the lane and headed up it, following the edge of the woods. A new-looking fence separated the track from the trees, and freshly cut stumps showed that it was being cleared for planting.

"Forestry," John muttered. "Won't do for us."

He tramped on up the track, with the girls following wearily behind. After a hundred paces they came to the end of the forestry fence. The track still climbed steeply upward, but now the slope on their right was thickly clad with old woodland, scrub oak and birch and hazel bushes growing from a tangle of briers and mossy rocks. John stopped at a place where it looked possible to clamber up into the woods and shuffled the knapsack off his shoulders.

"Take a rest," he said briefly. "I'm going to reconnoiter."

He dashed on up the track, while the girls flopped down in a patch of bracken and lay without speaking. They were too tired to talk. John was back in five minutes.

"All's well," he reported breathlessly. "Track comes out on open hillside — we'll go that way tomorrow. No farm anywhere in sight. Come on!"

He shouldered the knapsack and plunged through the bracken into a narrow gap in the trees. Ann and Ilonka followed him on what turned out to be a nightmare progress. It was quite dark in the woods, and the slope on which the trees stood consisted of loose rocks buried in leaf mold and hidden under knee-deep bracken and brambles. There seemed to be no flat places anywhere. In a few minutes the girls were panting and exhausted and John, under his weighty burden, was little better.

"Let's . . . stop and . . . just bivouac," gasped Ann at last.

"Bit farther yet," John grunted. "I've got a hunch."

He clambered across a miniature gully where a little stream trickled in a cleft, and groped his way up a pile of moss-grown boulders above it. A moment later the girls heard his exclamation of satisfaction. Hauling themselves up after him, they found him delightedly surveying a shelf or pocket of the woods. It was still light enough to see that the top edge of the boulder slope made a low rampart at the outer side of the shelf, which was about a dozen feet across, and behind it and on either side twisted oaks and hazel thickets formed a dense screen. It was a perfect hiding place.

"There isn't room for both tents." Ann, now scratched and sore as well as weary, spoke grumpily. "This bracken — "

"Then *make* room," John said quite sharply. "It'll soon be too dark to see, so get weaving. I'm relying on you two to pitch the tents while I sort out the supper."

Ann stopped grumbling and got to work. Ilonka, who hadn't spoken for some time, helped her without a word. Ann remembered that the older girl must be twice as tired as she was — to say nothing of her sore heel and damaged ankle. Whether she was a criminal or not — and Ann was sure she was on the run from something worse than an uncle — Ilonka was certainly game.

The dark burrow in the twilight forest was a grim and cheerless place, but in less than a quarter of an hour it was completely transformed. It was Home. John's small campfire had worked this miracle, turning the black thickets into a leafy wall of brown and gold and warming the toes of the three who sat around it eating baked beans piping hot from the pan. The tents, pitched close together and leaning rather drunkenly on the uneven ground, glowed with the ruddy light. The fire had been made with small dry hazel twigs, which burned clearly and well without producing any leaping flames or column of smoke; and, as John pointed out, even its reflected light could not be seen from the valley because of the rampart of boulders in front, and on the other three sides the thick screen of tree trunks and undergrowth hid it from all eyes but those of the pheasants and rabbits who lived deep in the wood. They were still hungry when the baked beans were finished, so John put some butter in the pan and made what he called an "omelette" with three eggs — a repulsive-looking mess which was polished off to the last fragment and voted delicious. After that they drank hot cocoa made with water from the stream in the gully. There was no milk to go with it, but with the extra sugar it was as good as anything they had ever tasted.

Then they just sat and talked, lolling on their couches of dry bracken.

Ilonka never forgot that camp in the woods. It was magical, the way her anxiety and weariness fell from her now that she was warm and full of food, safe in the charmed circle of firelight. She remembered afterward, when the adventures that awaited her were over, that this was the one really enjoyable hour. Even John's mutterings over the map, reminding her of the perils and chances of the long journey ahead, could not spoil her pleasure.

"We ought to camp well past Llangwm to-morrow," John meditated aloud. "There's the A494 to get over, but we can just nip across it and go straight over the hills. One more camp after that, and we're there."

Overhead the gap of night sky was as black as the trees outside their cave of firelight. A little wind whispered in the tree-tops and a leaf drifted down, changing to gold as it caught the glow from the fire.

"Pretty average good, this," John remarked.

Ilonka turned to look at him. She looked so contented that Ann wondered if her suspicions were after all unfounded.

"I think it's wonderful," she said, "how

you make yourself at home in a place like this, where probably no one's ever been before."

John tried not to look pleased with himself. "Well, I've done a bit of camping, you know," he said, "and so's Ann. It's all a matter of practice."

"And our usual practice," Ann murmured drowsily, "is to do the dishes right after a meal."

"Too dark now. Job for the women, first thing tomorrow." Her brother threw a last handful of twigs on the fire. "There's our candle. Let's turn in."

Ten minutes later the camp was dark and silent. The hot embers of the fire gave a sharp hiss, and then another. John, half asleep in his tent, heard a gentle tapping like elfin fingers on the tent fabric and knew that it was raining.

# The Fat Woman

ANN DAVIES had a grudging admiration
for Thomas Telford, who built the London-
to-Holyhead road a century and a half ago.
It was grudging because she wished there
were no roads thrusting into the gloriously
tangled hills and cwms (hollows) of North
Wales. But she couldn't help admiring his
route-finding — the way he had linked the
Dee valley and the Conway valley and the
deep trench of the Ogwen River to get his
coach road through the mountains to Ban-
gor. It was the A5 now, a stream of cars and
vans and long-distance trucks zooming along
the route that Telford had planned in the
reign of William IV; but the wild country

it passed through west of the Welsh Marches had hardly changed at all. During the first two days of their journey with Ilonka Kazinczy they were within five miles of the A5 all the time, and on these empty uplands it seemed impossible that a busy highway could be so close. On the first of the two days this had pleased Ann. Toward nightfall of the second day she would have given almost anything to find a road — even the A5 — under her boots. Their refuge, the lonely hills, had become a danger.

From morning, when they had started out wet from the forest camp, to evening when they found themselves on a bare and feature-less range of moorland hills, the rain had not stopped. In the deep glens it wasn't so bad, but on the ridges it was increasingly diffi-cult to face. It came driving out of the west, sweeping up the shelterless slopes like a charge of gray, ghostly cavalry, flattening the moor grass and rattling the spiky heath-er against their wet trousers. They were all soaked to the skin before noon, and — worse still — chilled to the bone. For they couldn't hold anything like the steady pace that would have kept their circulations going; Ilonka was only able to limp along slowly and painfully.

The Hungarian girl had managed fairly

well until they had passed what John called "the danger point" — the crossing of the A494 where it wound up a narrow glen. By ill fortune they had dropped out of the hillside thickets onto the road a few yards from where a gang of roadmen, in yellow oilskins, were sheltering from the driving rain. The men had waved to the three bedraggled hikers and one of them had shouted something. The rain must have hidden the three a minute after they had left the road by a gate on its farther side, and the roadmen could not have noted the course they took across the boggy glen and up the hillside beyond; but the fact that they had been seen appeared to bring Ilonka to the end of her courage. The ankle she had injured running down the lane above Llandrillo grew quickly worse. When they stopped for a hurried lunch of bread and cake and chocolate in a copse of dripping firs, John massaged the ankle, which looked red and swollen, and afterward insisted on carrying Ilonka's knapsack on top of his own, but from then on she had to walk at snail's pace and with frequent rests. Because John still hoped to get along the mountain crest above Llangwm and camp in some sheltered stream glen on the far side, they had pressed on stubbornly — only to find themselves lost on the high hills, with night upon them and the rain still driving relentlessly.

"John!"

Ann's urgent cry reached John, a dim gray figure plodding wearily ahead. He turned, and saw her standing above Ilonka, who had collapsed in a heap. Between them they helped her up. She was shivering so violently that she could hardly speak.

"I — I c-can't go on. I can't!"

John looked at Ann. Already it was so dark that he could only see her face as a pale blur. Wind and rain caught his words and hurled them at her in disjointed bits.

"That settles it . . . straight down . . . find shelter . . . farmhouse or something."

Ilonka heard that and started to protest. He shouted at her, his own voice shaking with the cold.

"We're two thousand feet up! People can die of exposure — we must find shelter and chance it. Must get off this ridge, anyway. Take her other arm, Ann!"

They gripped Ilonka between them and began to stumble across the uneven ground, heading now straight into the wind and rain. John's last look at his sodden map had shown him that the Llangwm valley lay somewhere below them on the west, and the rainstorm was blowing from due west. Unless they were even more lost than he thought, they should be able to drop down into that valley. After a hundred paces, to his great relief, the stony turf underfoot took a downward slant. Rain and the fast-gathering darkness hid everything in front, but soon they were descending a very steep hillside, dodging half-seen boulders and plunging into patches of mossy bog. Ilonka's ankle would not bear her weight at all, and they had to half drag, half carry her. When a dim star of light glimmered up at them from the dark void below, Ann was nearly exhausted and John was little better. They headed straight down for the yellow star, which gradually brightened until they could see through the blur of rain that it was the light from a curtained window. The outline of a building — cottage or small farmhouse — loomed close below. They felt the brief flatness of a track running across the hillside close above the house, stumbled against a stone wall and found a gate in it, and lurched down a few yards of path to the house. There was a door to the right of the bright square of window and John banged on it lustily. After a few moments it was opened, and the three soaked and weary travelers were blinking in the light that streamed past a massive figure standing on the threshold.

"And who might you be?" demanded a brisk voice, a woman's.

John, his lips blue and trembling with cold, started to stammer an explanation of their plight. The woman cut him short.

"Boy and two girls lost on the hills — one girl with injured ankle. That it?" She jerked out the words, a bit indistinctly because she had a cigarette in her mouth. "Bring her in. See what we can do. This way."

She led them into a brightly lit little room that was quite unlike a farmhouse parlor except for the floor of stone flags. Modern-looking chairs with gaudy cushions stood near a chromium electric fire; magazines and newspapers littered a seat beneath the curtained window; photographs on the newly painted walls showed groups of women in nurse's uniform. The big woman was replacing a policeman's truncheon — it had "V.R." painted on it in gold — among the other antiques that crowded the mantelpiece.

"Took it to the door just in case," she remarked, the cigarette waggling between her lips. "Live quite alone here — highest house in the valley. Never know, do you?"

Now that they could see her plainly, she seemed nearly as broad as she was tall, an enormously fat woman with frizzy gray hair and a face rather like a pig's except that it was red. She wore a bright-orange sweater and a tweed skirt. Two sharp little eyes surveyed the three dripping figures for a second before she spoke again in a commanding voice.

"Off with those sacks. Put 'em on the stones where they won't spoil my rugs. You, girl" — she pointed a finger like a sausage at Ann — "spread newspapers on that seat and sit on them. You, boy, take off this other wench's boot and socks. The damaged ankle, of course. Look sharp!"

She sounded so accustomed to being obeyed that they did what she told them at once. When John had removed the wet boot and soggy socks, she ordered Ilonka to lie flat on her back on the rug in front of the fire and quelled her feeble protests sharply.

"Shut up and do as I say! You've struck lucky, my girl, as you may find out in a minute. You all need a cup of tea, I know, but I'll deal with this ankle first. Then you can strip off and we'll find somewhere for you to sleep."

Ilonka was by this time stretched out on the rug, with little rivulets from her wet clothes soaking into it. The fat woman stubbed out her cigarette in an ash tray and got down on her knees at the girl's feet. Ann was lolling on the newspaper-covered seat with her eyes closed, letting the comforting warmth of the room revive her, but John was alert enough to notice what happened next. Ilonka had pushed back the hood of her drenched jacket, letting her bedraggled yellow hair escape. The fat woman's glance fell on it just as she was lifting the girl's bare foot into her lap, and for the space of a breath she stopped moving and knelt there rigid and staring. Almost at once, however, she began to speak.

"You needn't worry, dearie. Just relax — let this leg and foot go quite limp. I'm a nurse and I can find out what's wrong." As she talked she was waggling Ilonka's foot about gently, feeling its bones with her big fingers. "Think it's funny, a nurse living miles from anywhere in an old farm cottage? Well, I'm retired now. Always wanted a place like this. Had it done up — all modern conveniences and only twenty minutes from the village in my Mini. Local G.P. rings up now and then, so I get an occasional nursing job. This sort of job's a bit unusual, though — *ah!*"

They all heard the "click" as she gave Ilonka's foot a sudden deft wrench. Ilonka squeaked with pain, and Ann — who had sat up to watch what was going on — looked a bit frightened. The fat woman got to her feet, rubbing her hands together with a satisfied air.

"Thank your stars I did a spell with an osteopath, dearie," she said, sounding very pleased with herself. "Small bone dislocated — I've put it back for you. Stand up. Go on! Put your weight on that foot."

She lit another cigarette while Ilonka, rather doubtfully, obeyed. An expression of surprise and pleasure grew on the Hungarian girl's face.

"Why — the sharp pain's gone!" she exclaimed. "It aches and feels awfully stiff —"

"Bound to. Night's rest'll put that right, even though you'll have to sleep on my floor. Plenty of blankets. Now get in front of that fire, all of you," she added, cutting short the thanks which John and Ilonka both started to utter. "You're steaming already, but I don't mind the stink. I'm going to put a kettle on."

She went out through an inner door, shutting it firmly behind her. Ilonka began to try out her ankle, walking slowly up and down the room. Ann looked at John.

"Well!" she said. "This is really choice! We get lost, find a lonely cottage — and there's a fairy godmother waiting for us, complete with magic to cure Ilonka's foot."

"We weren't actually *lost*," John objected. "Of course, we were forced to get off the hills pretty quick, but another hour and a half along that ridge and we could have — "

"*Ss-sh!*" hissed Ilonka suddenly.

Her trial walking had brought her close to the door by which the fat woman had gone out. She was bending down close to it and beckoning urgently to the others to come and listen. They tiptoed across and got their ears near the panels. The fat woman was talking to someone in a low voice — and she had told them she was alone in the cottage.

" . . . I know the line's bad, but I don't want to speak louder. . . . "

The telephone, of course. She had said the local G.P. sometimes rang her up. But no telephone bell had rung, so she had made the call herself. Her voice went on.

"Yes . . . three of 'em, but the girl's blond and about fifteen, I'd say . . . Look here, Inspector, you know very well I can't be dead certain . . . all right, I'll hold 'em till you . . . "

That was all they heard, because Ilonka drew John and Ann away from the door. Her face was pale, but set in a look of fierce determination.

"I'm getting my boot on at once," she whispered rapidly. "She told the police, and there's not a minute to spare."

"But how on earth did she know?" Ann demanded in a low voice. "And where are we to go from here?"

John gripped her arm. "Never mind that — we'll find shelter somewhere. They can't find us on a night like this. Stand by the fire, like she said . . . "

He stopped and took a quick pace forward to screen Ilonka, who was already dragging on her wet socks. The door opened and the fat woman put in her head. For the first time since she had let them in she was grinning all over her big red face — and it was a horribly false grin. Ann thought she looked more like a witch than a fairy godmother now.

"Tea in five minutes, dearies," she announced. "Hot buttered scones, do you?"

"Fine," answered John, forcing himself to smile back at her. "It's really awfully kind of you — "

"Not a word. Pleasure's mine."

The head vanished. The door was shut again. Ilonka finished the hurried lacing of her boot and stood up. John put a warning finger to his lips and picked up his knapsack; the others took their sacks and followed him to the outer door of the cottage. The click as he lifted the latch made them all jump guiltily, but there was no sound from inside the house. Two minutes later they were tramping through the rain and darkness again, following the grass track that ran on the hillside just above the fat woman's cottage.

They moved silently and fast, John leading the way. Behind him Ilonka tramped gently, though her ankle was still stiff and swollen and caused her to limp. Ann, bringing up the rear, trudged miserably at first. The chill wet wind made her shiver in her damp clothes after the warmth of the room and she felt that leaving the firelight and shelter — not to mention hot buttered scones — was just silly, even if staying would have meant Ilonka having to go back to Uncle Zoltan. But *was* that all it would have meant? The fat woman in her remote hill cottage had known that Ilonka was the girl wanted by the police. Didn't that show that there was a really wide search on, something much bigger than an uncle trying to recover a runaway niece?

A roaring noise ahead of them banished these thoughts from Ann's mind with a jerk; but it was only a stream tumbling down the invisible hillside on their left. The track crossed it by a narrow bridge of stone slabs and went on, keeping more or less level. It was too dark to see their surroundings at all, but they seemed to be rounding the sides of a big cwm. Wind and rain had slackened a little and the quick movement had brought a little warmth to their bodies in spite of their soaking clothes when they saw another yellow gleam down in the darkness on their right. As she spotted it, Ann bumped into Ilonka, who had stopped. John had halted under the wall of some sort of building and was sniffing the wet air.

"Hay!" he said in a whisper. "This'll do us! But don't make a row — there's a farmhouse not far below."

He pushed at a rickety wooden door and it opened, letting them into sweet-scented darkness. The hay was piled to the roof of the barn at one end, but at the other end some of it had been used, leaving a sort of platform of hay five feet above the stone floor. They took off their knapsacks and scrambled up to burrow deep into the dry and tickly stuff. By the time John had produced a slice of bread and butter and some chocolate by way of supper, Ann was nearly too sleepy to eat it. The warmth of the hay was making her wet things almost comfortable. The last thing she heard was John telling Ilonka that they were safe as houses here but must get away at first light next morning. Then she was asleep.

When she woke it was still pitch-dark in the barn and John was shaking her by the shoulder.

"Hot cocoa," he muttered. "Ilonka's had hers."

"Choice!" Ann exclaimed, taking the mug from him and sipping gratefully. "How did you manage it?"

"Not so loud. Stream a hundred yards away across the hillside, matches still dry in waterproof packing. I used the solid-fuel stove. Get weaving — it's stopped raining and it's light enough to move."

He crawled down off the hay. Just below, Ann could hear steady footsteps going across the stone floor and back; Ilonka was testing her ankle for the day's tramp. When Ann got down to the floor herself she found she was very stiff and aching all over, so she did a few exercises to limber up. She had slept warmly in the hay, but her clothes were still very damp and she felt cold the moment they stepped outside into the gray morning light. John had a cure for that. He led them on a slanting course up the steep hillside above the barn, and soon the blood was racing in their veins and warming them to the finger-tips.

Rain and wind had gone and the dank morning air was perfectly still. Mist lay in flat gray swathes over the dark valley below them, where fields and trees were just beginning to show their colors. Low clouds, ribbed like a pattern of wool on a gray sweater, hung across the sky, and when they topped the crest of the ridge and could look eastward, they saw the purple-red stain of sunrise seeping upward into the gray like blackberry juice.

John licked his forefinger and held it up to catch the faint drift of wind. "Veered right around to nor'-nor'-east," he announced nautically. "Fine day coming."

That was the beginning of a surprisingly cheerful day. Though all their belongings were wet, though they never quite lost the feeling of a net closing around them, their spirits rose with the rising sun. They tramped westward along the undulating crest for an hour, startling the sheep from their wet beds in hollows of the stony turf, and Ilonka strode as swiftly and steadily as her companions. The sun blinked briefly at them as it rose over the distant Berwyn crests, and a few minutes later John halted on a bald summit covered with stones and took off his knapsack.

"Breakfast," he announced. "Bread, last of the cheese, half a bar of chocolate each. That leaves fruit cake and chocolate for lunch — I'll have to buy food for supper somehow."

He spread out his damp and battered map. The girls, munching, looked over his shoulder while — between mouthfuls — he expounded the day's route.

"If we follow the ridge northwest and drop down west where it ends, we'll cross a lane and take this old drove track northward. It joins another hill track that crosses to the hills above a place called Yspytty Ifan. In those hills we'll find a good safe place to camp." He turned to Ilonka. "About twelve miles — think you can make it?"

"Easily, if this ankle goes on as it's begun. That fat woman slipped up badly, putting it right before she phoned the police, so I'm thankful twice over." She craned across him to peer at the map. "How far after this Spitty place?"

John grinned. "Yspytty Ifan. It means some medieval type named Evan used to keep a hospice there. 'Bout fourteen miles

94

still to go from there, so with an early start we'll be at journey's end before sunset tomorrow."

Overhead the gray woolly clouds were breaking and blue sky showed through the gaps. Ann, glancing at Ilonka, surprised a curious expression on her face — a mingling of apprehension and something like shame. Then a golden lance of sunshine broke slanting through the clouds, and the shadow vanished from Ilonka's face as her own shadow fell on the ground. She stretched out her arms to the sun.

"Make haste while the sun shines!" She laughed. "With you two on my side, I feel I really *am* going to get safely to Croesor."

# Hare and Hounds

It was a quarter to five, teatime, when John started down from the camp site to buy food in the village of Yspytty Ifan. He felt he was leaving a secure fortress and making a foray into the enemy's camp.

He had discovered that perfect site partly by luck and partly by skillful use of the One-Inch map. The rolling moorland hills they had crossed that day, meeting no one but a shepherd and his two dogs, fell on the west into the deep upper glen of the River Conway, and a small tributary stream had cut into the upper slopes of grass and rock to form a miniature canyon. At its back was a fifteen-foot wall of rock clothed thickly with ivy, down which the water trickled sparkling in the afternoon sunshine to form a pool between the reedy banks of the ravine; on the left bank was a level platform of turf like a quay, just big enough to hold the two tents; rowans and hazels made a screen of golden leaves and glowing red berries at the outer end of the little canyon, which looked out across the valley five hundred feet below. The westering sun struck straight into this ideal hiding place. There were plenty of hazel twigs and old ivy wood, dry after the day of sun and wind, and though a fire might be seen from the valley after dark, it was safe enough to light one in daylight. The one thing they were short of was food. Except for cocoa, sugar, and a little butter, they had finished all their provisions when they lunched at noon in the head of the Ceirw glen. Leaving Ann and Ilonka puttering about in bare feet and spreading out their things to dry in the last of the sun, John set forth on his foraging expedition.

Since ten o'clock the sky had been cloudless, with a brisk northerly wind that had dried their clothes on them as they walked, and the stone-walled fields on the lower hillside were still bathed in golden light as he dodged cautiously down, keeping close to the walls. The river valley was already in the shadow of the wooded western hills, with the Conway showing a dull glint of silver below the rich autumn colors of its fringing trees. There was a farmhouse in sight up the valley to the left, and a narrow road came snaking down beside the river from high brown moorland hills in the west — the hills they would have to cross tomorrow. To the right the white and gray cottages of Yspytty Ifan stood on the east bank of the river half a mile away. John was making for a footbridge which, according to his map, crossed the Conway just above the road bridge leading to the village. He intended to enter Yspytty Ifan, and leave it, on the western side, so that no one could suspect he came from a camp on the hills to eastward. He reached the footbridge — a wooden structure amid trees — and crossed the swirling river to the road on the other side. He had seen no one, and the driver of a car that sped past as he emerged into the road paid no attention to him. There was, after all, no reason why anyone should notice a solitary hiker making an autumn walking tour in Wales.

John was taking no chances. The affair of the fat woman had shown that there was an intensive search on for Ilonka Kazinczy; by now the searchers would know that there were three fugitives and that they were heading westward across the hills. He was puzzled by this and a little dismayed, but concluded that Ilonka's Uncle Zoltan must have even more influence than his niece had suggested. Even Uncle Zoltan, however, couldn't have arranged for more than a fraction of the Welsh police to search for them. It was unlikely, he had decided, that there was a policeman in a tiny place like Yspytty Ifan and more unlikely still that anyone would connect a lone walker with the party of three that had disappeared from the fat woman's cottage. All the same, he had to gulp down his nervousness as he turned to the right over the old stone bridge and entered the village.

Yspytty Ifan was just a broad, grass-bordered street with a dozen cottages on each side. It was anything but quiet, though; half a dozen children were shrieking in Welsh as they played some complicated game near the end of the bridge, a flock of sea gulls were quarreling on a refuse heap behind the cottages, and three dogs were barking like mad. The sight of the sea gulls reminded John that the sea was now less than twenty miles away. He walked on confidently. One of the cottages displayed a board with the words YSPYTTY POST OFFICE. A small car stood outside it. Opposite was the only shop, a very small place claiming to be GROCER but looking, to John's relief, as if it sold most things. He went in, by doing so quite filling the shop although there was only one other customer there, a stout farmer buying cigarettes and talking Welsh to the elderly woman behind the counter. They both smiled pleasantly at John and said "Good afternoon." Then the farmer went out and John gave his order — one loaf of bread, a package of wrapped cheese, a box of cookies, a large can of oxtail soup, six bars of plain chocolate, a small fruit cake, a box of matches. The woman started to collect these from various corners of the shop while he looked at the goods displayed in the window. There was a bunch of bananas there, and they could do with some fruit. He had just decided to buy three when he happened to raise his eyes and look through the window to the opposite side of the road.

Two men had come out of the post office and were standing by the car, and both of them were staring at the shop window. One was a little man in a cloth cap; the other was much taller, with no hat on his thick gray hair. John felt his memory give a sort of twitch. When his glance took in the car as well as the tall gray-haired man, he knew what the twitch meant, for the car was a green Morris convertible.

Forty-eight hours ago, crouching in the lane beyond Llandrillo, he had seen that car go past with its top down, and this same gray-haired man had been standing up in it admiring the scenery — or, just possibly, looking for Ilonka Kazinczy.

John's thoughts raced. Just a coincidence? More likely it wasn't. The men didn't look like plainclothesmen, and yet — suppose they had made inquiries in Llandrillo that day. They'd have easily discovered that three hikers had left by the Bala road. They'd have followed in the car, trying to spot whether the three had turned off anywhere. Of course they'd lost the trail, but— knowing the fugitives' direction — they would watch the roads and villages on that westerly course and so had turned up here. That fitted only too well. It was sheer bad luck —

"Is there anything else?" asked the shop woman.

"Three bananas, please," John said absently, still looking through the window.

The gray-haired man was coming across

the road, straight for the shop. He came in just as the woman wrapped the bananas up in a sheet of newspaper. John handed her money and began to push the packages into his empty knapsack as fast as he could.

"You'll be camping near here," said the woman, giving him the change.

John had to answer. "Yes," he said briefly.

The gray-haired man bought a box of matches and then turned to speak to him. He had a deep harsh voice and he sounded like a foreigner.

"Doubtless it is your task to buy the supper for your fellow campers," he remarked genially. "It is surely late in the year for camping. Are there many of you, may I ask?"

John looked up from cramming the paper-wrapped bananas on top of the other things. He saw a brown hawklike face crinkled in a smile, and two steel-gray eyes that didn't smile at all.

"Oh no," he replied quickly. "I'm on my own."

"Indeed? And where is your tent? For I see you have not it with you."

" 'Bout a mile from here." John was thinking furiously, trying to remember the map. "I was — I was walking over from Festiniog by the old tracks. I found a good place, up on the hillside west of here, so I pitched the tent and came down to get some food." He tied the laces of the knapsack hurriedly. "Must get on — be dark soon. Good evening!"

He slipped past the gray-haired man and got outside. The man in the cloth cap was still standing by the car. John started to walk fast toward the bridge without looking at him, surer than ever that these two were hunting Ilonka — friends or servants of Uncle Zoltan, perhaps. He had told the best lies he could, but he had a horrible feeling that some of them hadn't been believed. When he had crossed the hump of the bridge he shot a quick glance over his shoulder. The two men were standing together in the roadway, talking. To all appearances they were taking no notice of him, but from there they could see which way he turned on the road — so he mustn't turn that way. At the junction, directly opposite the side road leading to Yspytty Ifan, a steep and stony cart track slanted up the hillside between hedges of thorn and hazel. John crossed the valley road and went straight on up this track, thus heading in the opposite direction to the one he must take to get back to the ravine camp.

The thick hedge and the scrub oaks below it screened him from the village, and he halted to peer down at the bridge. The two men were coming across it, and coming fast. There could be no doubt that they intended to follow him.

As he toiled on up the mounting track, John made himself work it out methodically. These men couldn't know he had seen them before. They would expect him to cover up when he was asked about his companions, because they would assume he was helping Ilonka to escape from her pursuers and would tell nobody who was with him; but they wouldn't know he had lied about the whereabouts of his campsite. So his first job was to convince them that the camp really was somewhere up on this western hillside. After that, he had to disappear completely and return to the ravine camp without giving the slightest indication where he had gone. It wasn't going to be easy.

The track climbed above the trees and ran between stone walls instead of hedges. A lumpy hill straight ahead rose against a sky glowing with the orange light of sunset, and the slopes across the valley on his left were shadowed now; he hoped Ann would have sense enough to let the fire go out before darkness fell. A gate — he passed through it on to open hillside. So far he hadn't once glanced behind him. The two men had to think he didn't know they were on his trail. But now, as he followed the winding grassy track through a maze of rocky hills and reedy hollows, he strained his ears and was rewarded by hearing the faint click of the gate. They were about a hundred yards behind him, then, and no doubt they intended to follow, keeping just out of sight. In this moorland wilderness of humps and dips that should be easy for them, but somehow he had to dodge off the track and leave them still thinking — for a time, at any rate — that he was on ahead.

John felt all his senses sharpened by excitement, as they had been, he remembered, when he had been one of the two Hares in a school game of Hare and Hounds. In this case, though, the Hounds were not out to catch him until he'd led them to their real quarry. The thought that Ilonka's fate depended on him put an edge of anxiety on his excitement.

The way curled up to a notch in a heathery rise from which he could see some distance ahead up the hillside. Below him the track dropped slightly and rounded a patch of marsh before vanishing behind a low shoulder of hill. So far as could be seen, it didn't reappear until it emerged on a bare grass slope several hundred feet above. He wasn't likely to find a better place than this. He walked steadily downhill until he was sure he was out of sight from behind and then leaped to the left off the track and went racing along the flank of the low heathery ridge with the marsh close on his right. He made a good fifty yards before dropping flat behind a two-foot bush of heather with his heart pounding like a pneumatic drill. By raising his head a little he could look through the screen of heather twigs toward the track.

The Hounds didn't appear for half a minute or more; evidently they were approaching the rise cautiously in case the Hare was still in sight beyond it. Then he saw them — or their upper halves, for the heather hid their legs — walking quickly along until they passed out of sight around the shoulder of the hill.

John waited no longer. Bent almost double, he crept downhill through the heather, placing his feet with care to avoid making noise, until he reached a slope of pasture grass. Then he ran at top speed with the knapsack bumping uncomfortably on his back, sprinting for a stone wall lower down the pasture. The gate by which the track passed through this wall was some distance uphill to the left, but though John had used the hare's trick of doubling on his tracks he had no intention of returning by the way he had come; it was just possible that the two men might discover quickly that he was no longer in front and race back to the gate. He turned right when he reached the wall, and ran along it until it dipped below a reed-covered mound. From behind the reeds he took a long look at the skyline above him, where his pursuers would appear if they had guessed where he had gone. Nothing stirred there. He turned and climbed carefully over the wall.

As he expected, the ground fell away very steeply on the other side, straight down to the road along the Conway glen. Tall bracken tangled with a mass of brambles made even downhill going difficult as far as a belt of woodland, but here it was merely a matter of steering a course between the tree trunks and avoiding sharp branches that stabbed at his eyes like witches' fingernails. Twilight darkened the wood and it was a witchcrafty sort of place. Once, when he stopped to listen for sounds of pursuit, there came a sudden and noisy clatter from close overhead that startled him as though it had been a gunshot. A moment later he was telling himself contemptuously that a kid would have known instantly it was wood pigeons disturbed from their roosting place. No one could have followed him down that slope without making a lot of noise, and there was no noise of that kind. He descended the last few yards to the fence bordering the road.

A car was droning up the hill from Yspytty Ifan. He waited until its red rear light was well past before getting over the fence onto the road. He had reached it only fifty paces from the footbridge across the Conway, and the ravine camp was an easy half hour away up the slopes on the farther side.

John lost no time in getting off the road and down the short path to the footbridge. Purple gloaming hung in the thickets of the river glen, and the water bumbling and chuckling under the narrow bridge was dark. But behind him the steep flank he had just descended reared its crest against a sky that glowed with clear lemon-yellow light, so that although it was past lighting-up time the western-facing mountain slopes still showed their detail. He changed his mind about going straight up to the ravine camp.

By now the Hounds had probably discovered the Hare's trickery, and those steel-gray eyes — he remembered their keen glance — might be sweeping every hillside in sight. He was pleased with the success of his tactics — pretty average good, in his opinion — and felt certain the pursuit was well and truly baffled; but one glimpse of a moving figure on those slopes would put them on the trail again. It was better to wait by the river for half an hour, until the after-sunset light had faded and the hillside was dark and safe.

The footbridge was rickety and looked disused, but he decided to get into cover in case anyone should come along the path. A few yards downstream a cluster of stunted oaks spread their branches low above the riverside boulders. He was creeping under these when a branch hooked itself into the loosened strings of his knapsack and tilted it over his ears, sending the newspaper-wrapped bananas pitching onto the boulders. He rescued them before they could roll into the water and started to wrap them up again in the paper. It was the front page of a daily newspaper, two days old, with one corner torn off close to the picture of a girl with some heavy lettering beneath it. The photograph was unusually clear. The girl in the picture was Ilonka.

Half the printing beneath it had been torn away, but what remained could be read by the fading sunset light:

### HAVE YOU SEEN THIS GIRL?

*She is 15-year-old Ilonka Kazinc*
*a pretty blonde, wanted by t*
*police in connection wi*
*murder of Zoltan Mel*
*days ago in a Lon*
*She is thought*
*hills of N*
*but may*
*If*

The twilight chill of the darkening glen seemed to strike into John's very bones as his eyes came back to that one ugly word: MURDER.

# Ilonka Tells the Truth

THE FIRST STAR was glinting in a pale blue-green sky when John reached the little ravine. The camp was dark except for a very faint glow near the rock wall, where Ann and Ilonka were crouched over the hot embers of the fire toasting their damp socks. Both girls greeted the returned forager with relief and abandoned their sock-drying to examine the things he emptied out of his sack.

"We're practically starving," Ann declared. "Where on earth have you been — and what have you got?"

"We were getting really worried, John," said Ilonka. "Ann even thought of going to look for you."

John grunted and rummaged in his tent for the solid-fuel stove.

"Oxtail soup — oh, choice!" Ann was peering at the various packages. "That's for supper, with chunks of bread. Then fruit cake and cookies, and cheese if required. Banana each for afters. Is that the menu, John?"

"Yes," said her brother tersely. "Get on and open that can. I've got to light this stove."

Something in his voice and manner alarmed Ann. John was sometimes a bit overbearing, but never snappy or surly.

"What's the matter?" she demanded. "Has something happened?"

John went on preparing the stove without answering her. Then he pulled out the newspaper, which he had folded and put in his pocket, and squatted in the doorway of the larger tent, where Ilonka was sitting and cutting bread.

"*This* has happened," he said.

He flicked on the tiny beam of his pencil flashlight and held it so that Ilonka could read the printed words. Ann, who had come close to peer at the newspaper, drew in her breath with a sharp hissing sound. The Hungarian girl stiffened and sat like a statue.

"*Istenem!*" she whispered.

There was a little silence. The music of the stream tumbling down the rock wall seemed unnaturally loud. Ilonka spoke at last.

"I'm glad you found this, John," she said quietly. "I've felt awful, deceiving you and Ann all this — "

"It's true, then!" Ann broke in. "You *did* lie to us, the night we hid you!"

Ilonka put out a hand appealingly. "I had to — don't you see? I couldn't expect you to hide me if you knew — this."

"You swore you hadn't committed a crime!"

"Nor I have, Ann. I'm 'wanted in connection with,' that's all."

"That could mean anything!"

"In my opinion," John said slowly, "this bit in the paper explains one or two things. It explains why Ilonka's being hunted so hard. It explains why the fat woman phoned the police as soon as she recognized her — she'd seen this paper, of course. I was wondering as I came up the hill," he added even more slowly, "if it wasn't my duty to go back to the village and phone the police myself."

"Is that so!" Ilonka sprang to her feet,

scattering loaf, knife, and slices of bread. "You believe I'm a murderess, no doubt — right!" She sounded furious. "You stay on the side of the Law, John Davies — I'm leaving you to it, here and now!"

She swung on her heel and strode away toward the end of the ravine. This dramatic exit was spoiled, however, when she tripped over a rock and fell flat on her face. John jumped up and pulled her to her feet.

"Don't be a silly goose, Ilonka," he said severely. "You can't get to Croesor without any boots on."

For some reason this remark so amused Ann that she spluttered with laughter, while Ilonka squeaked with the pain of her injured toes.

"It's no laughing matter," John snapped.

"I know," faltered Ilonka. "There's nothing hurts so much as stubbing your — "

"I was talking to Ann!"

John almost roared the words. And then he too was suddenly overtaken by laughter. Ilonka, rubbing her toes, started to chuckle. But it was she who called them to order.

"This is just silly," she said reasonably. "I *am* in a tighter jam than I told you, and it *is* your duty to give me up to the police. But I haven't committed a crime — unless dodging the police is one — and I'd like to explain if you'll let me. I swear it will be the whole truth this time," she added.

"Good," said John. "But we ought to get on with supper. It was being hungry that made us bark at each other like we did just now."

Ann groped for the bread. "I'll do the cutting," she said. "I've opened the can. You brew the soup, John, and Ilonka can concentrate on telling the truth. It'll be nice to know what we've let ourselves in for."

"I'm awfully sorry, Ann," Ilonka said, sitting down beside her again. "I gave my word to keep it absolutely secret. This morning, at sunrise, I nearly broke my word and told you — and now I'm going to do it. Here it comes, the whole story."

A faint wind moved the branches of the rowans, fluttering the black silhouettes of the leaves against the peeping stars. Like a nearer star, the blue flame of the stove glimmered under the pan of soup, which John was stirring slowly. Ann was cutting slices from the loaf, no easy job in the darkness. With the ceaseless chatter of the stream for accompaniment, Ilonka began her story.

"A lot of what I told you that first night was true. My parents really are dead, and Uncle Zoltan Melich is — I mean was — my guardian. I hated him. He wasn't really cruel

115

to me, but just — well, horrid. So was the woman he called his housekeeper. Her name was Anna and I think she was Russian. Uncle Zoltan had a creepy, slinky sort of way with him and seemed to be always afraid of something. About a fortnight ago a burglar tried to get into the house — it was in a fairly quiet part of London — and after that Uncle Zoltan was really scared, I thought. One night last week he fetched me down from my room upstairs, where I was doing my homework, and took me into his study. He locked the door, got out a Bible, and told me to swear on the Bible that I wouldn't tell a soul the things he was going to tell me now. He said the lives of hundreds of true Hungarians depended on it, so of course I swore."

John stopped his stirring. "Look," he said uncomfortably, "if you think you ought not to break your oath — "

"But I've got to, if I'm to carry out my mission. I've learned that I can't do that without your help."

"This journey of yours is a mission, then?" Ann said.

"Yes. You'll understand in a moment. Well, Uncle Zoltan told me then that for a long time he'd been working with a secret Hungarian organization in Britain, called

Free Hungary. It was planning another revolution to overthrow Soviet rule, and corresponding with underground agents in Hungary itself. If the British police found out about it, he said, it would be disbanded and all the work would be in vain. But the worst danger was from Communist agents in Britain, who would give anything to know which of the Hungarian refugees were members of Free Hungary."

"He'd know, I suppose, that you'd be on the side of Free Hungary," John interposed.

"He knew that, of course," Ilonka agreed. "The surprise for me was to discover that *he* was in such a plot, and up to his neck too. He went on to tell me that for better security only one man knew the names and addresses of the London Hungarians who were working against the Soviet. He was that man. Then he unlocked the safe in the study wall and got out a small packet wrapped in brown paper — Just a second."

She wriggled around and rummaged in the back of the tent to get something out of her knapsack. Ann remembered how careful Ilonka had been to keep the knapsack fastened, and how she always used it as a pillow at night. She remembered too, feeling a parcel wrapped in paper when she was getting out Ilonka's pajamas that first night.

"This is it." Ilonka was holding a package the size of a small book. "It's too dark to see, but there's a name and address on it in pencil. I know it by heart — Gyula Zichy, Ty Gwyn, Croesor, North Wales."

"That's your Uncle Gyula, your father's brother?" Ann asked.

"That was part of the story I thought up to tell you and John. No — I'd never heard of this Gyula before. Uncle Zoltan told me his name was Gyula Zichy and he was a top man in the Free Hungary organization. He was an artist and lived in this cottage in the mountains. In the packet was a book, full of information about all the Free Hungary agents in Britain. If anything happened to him, Uncle Zoltan said, I was to take the packet and carry it myself to Gyula Zichy. I wasn't to hand it to anyone else or let anyone know I was doing this."

"But why you?" John wanted to know. "Why not one of these Free Hungary agents?"

"That's what I asked him," Ilonka nodded. "I didn't much like the idea. He said he knew I'd like to do a great service for my country and he'd decided I could be trusted. Anna hadn't enough sense, and any of the Free Hungary men might be suspected and followed. I asked him too what he thought

118

might happen to him. He looked very scared and muttered something about being taken ill or having to go away suddenly. But then he quite broke down and said his life was being threatened — the men who had tried to break in were out to get the packet at all costs and would kill him to get it. He begged me to give him my solemn promise that I'd do as he asked."

"And you had to, really, he being your uncle," said Ann.

"Yes. Anyway, I did. Then he unlocked the door that led into the hall, and we listened. We could hear Anna snoring. Uncle Zoltan unscrewed the wooden top of the post at the bottom of the stairs and showed me a secret hiding place he'd made himself. He put the packet in it and screwed the top on again. I was only to take it out, he said, if something happened like he'd been telling me. In that case I must get away instantly — he stuck his face close to mine and repeated, *'instantly'* — with the packet, and carry it to Gyula Zichy as fast as possible."

"Well, you haven't gone very fast up to now," John commented; he blew out the stove. "Soup's ready — can you go on talking while you eat?"

Ilonka said eagerly that she could, so he filled the two big enamel mugs for the girls and ate out of the pan himself. They dipped the thick slices of bread Ann had cut into the delicious-smelling stuff, and for a minute or two the story had to wait while they satisfied their hunger. Ann was glad she had the comforting food inside her when she heard Ilonka's next words.

"Two nights later Uncle Zoltan was murdered." The girl paused. "I won't forget that night, ever. I woke up with a start, and heard Anna screaming downstairs. It was nearly midnight. I rushed down and there she was yelling and pointing to the study door, which was open. I looked in, and saw the wall safe open and Uncle Zoltan lying on the floor. He was dead. His — the blood — well, it was just horrible."

She gulped and shuddered. John put in a word to give her time to recover.

"This was the night before you came to our camp in the Ceiriog valley. Is that right?"

"Yes." Ilonka waggled her shoulders, shaking off the memory of what she had seen. "Anna had seen no one — whoever did it had got away. The thing Uncle Zoltan had been afraid of had happened, and it was up to me to keep my promise. The telephone was in the study, so I pushed her in there and told her to phone the police at once. As soon as I heard her dialing I got the packet from its hiding place and rushed upstairs. This skiing outfit was handy, so I put it on. I got all the money I had, put some things in a knapsack, and got out by the back door without Anna seeing me. Just as I reached the street, a police car dashed up and stopped outside the house."

"Goodness! Didn't they stop you?"

Ann, who had finished her soup, shot out the question excitedly. Ilonka patted her knee reassuringly.

"A man asked me some questions, but I told him I lived at the other end of the street and he let me go."

"But they'd soon find out who you were by questioning Anna," John said. "And of course that's why there's a big search on for you — you cleared off, and lied to the police on the way, right after the murder. What did you do next?"

"Made tracks for Euston Station. But it was after midnight now, and there wasn't a train going anywhere near North Wales until the eleven-ten. I found out I could change at a junction and then get a train to a place called Llanrwst. There was a railway map by the booking office and it looked from that as though I wouldn't be far from Croesor there."

"You'd have been twenty or thirty miles away," growled John. "But you didn't get to Llanrwst."

"No. Things happened to prevent me. I was being followed."

"The police?"

Ilonka shook her head. "I don't think they got after me until later. This was a man I caught a glimpse of outside the inquiry office — I'd gone there from the booking office, and I remembered noticing him outside that too. I wandered about the station for a bit wondering how to fill in the time, and I didn't see him again. But I kept spotting another man, a small thin man in a cloth cap. I was sure he was watching me."

"Little man in cloth cap?" repeated John. "What was the other man like?"

"Like the man you saw in the car near Llandrillo — tall with a lot of gray hair. Why?"

John grunted. "Tell you later. What did you do about these followers?"

"I was awfully frightened," Ilonka admitted. "I felt certain they weren't policemen — they didn't look English — and I remembered what Uncle Zoltan had said about Communist agents badly wanting the packet. The packet was there in my knapsack, you know. I tried frantically to think of a way of shaking them off — and then I had a wonderful piece of luck. I found myself by the place where the taxis wait, and the only car in sight was one solitary taxi. I had plenty of money, so I jumped in and told him to take me to Spaniards Road, which runs across the high part of Hampstead Heath. When I got there I went on to the Heath and found a place to sit down in some bushes until morning."

"You poor thing!" Ann squeezed Ilonka's hand, which was still resting on her knee. "I'd have been scared stiff."

Ilonka returned the squeeze gratefully. "So was I. But all that happened was that I got a bit wet — and I *was* stiff, and still scared, in the morning. I walked about on the Heath to unstiffen and then got a bus in the Highgate Road. I was back at Euston with just time to have a cup of tea and a cake and catch the eleven-ten."

"And you got on the train without those men spotting you?" Ann demanded breathlessly.

"Not quite. Look — I'm nearly at the end of the story, but I'm getting hoarse. And I'll be awfully thirsty in a minute."

John got to his feet. "Right — interval for

preparing second course. You and Ann wash the mugs and cut some fruit cake, while I scour the pan and start brewing cocoa."

They set to work at these tasks almost in silence. Ann could hardly wait to hear the rest of the story, even though she knew that Ilonka hadn't been caught — not yet, at any rate. John frowned to himself over his scouring; he was thinking that what he had just heard turned their holiday escapade into a much more dangerous affair. As for Ilonka, her thoughts were back at the Euston ticket barrier when she had walked up to it with her heart in her mouth. When the pan was on the stove again and they were all sitting down with a piece of fruit cake to nibble, she plunged straight into her tale.

"There was no sign of the two men, and no one near the barrier looked like a policeman. I got into a carriage just before the train pulled out. There were five quite ordinary people in the carriage and I began to feel safe."

"Funny," John remarked. "The police must have been slow getting after you."

"Yes. I was too thankful to worry about them. I sat back and dozed a bit until the train made its first stop — at Leamington, I think it was. I was looking out of the window when a man came walking quickly along the platform. It was the tall gray-haired man I'd seen at Euston. He saw me — I was sure of that — but he just walked straight past and I guessed he was checking that I was still on the train. I didn't know what to do. I had to change at Wolverhampton and you can bet I looked out for him there, but I didn't see him until I was in the other train. I had a corner seat on the platform side, with my back to the engine, and just as the train started to move I saw two men dash out from a waiting room and jump into a carriage at the rear of the train. One was the gray-haired man and the other was the little man in the cloth cap."

"Good grief!" John muttered. "You certainly were in a spot. I wouldn't have known what to do."

"Nor did I," Ilonka confessed, "until I remembered a mystery I'd seen on television. It seemed a corny old trick, but I had to try it. When the train started to slow for the next stop I went along the corridor and found an empty first-class carriage. The moment it stopped I got out on the wrong side — climbed down onto the line — and crept along to the back of the train and up to the end of the platform."

Ann shivered. "Suppose a train had come on the other line!"

"I thought of that, all right — but I was pretty desperate, you know. Some people on the opposite platform saw me, but no one shouted or anything and the train pulled out while I was hidden behind a trolley piled with crates. Then I walked out of the station. It was a place called Gobowen. The ticket collector wanted to know why I'd got off there instead of going on and I had quite a job to get away from him. Almost the first thing I saw in the streets of Gobowen was a policeman, and I was so jumpy by this time that I ran for a bus that was just leaving the town square and got aboard. It was a local bus, only going as far as Chirk — three miles."

"And north of Gobowen," John put in. "You needed to go west from Gobowen."

"I did," Ilonka nodded. "And I discovered that, from a map in the bus that showed the routes. When I got out at Chirk I went into a grocer's shop by the bus stop and they told me there wasn't a bus to Glyn Ceiriog — which was the way I'd decided to go — until hours later. But their van was going there almost at once and could give me a lift. And that," she ended, "is my true story. When the van set me down in Glyn Ceiriog I started to walk up the valley in the twilight, saw the police car coming behind me, and dodged into your camp. That was lucky for me — but you'll say it wasn't very lucky for you."

"Oh, rubbish!" Ann said impulsively. "You deserve to win after all that — and we'll help you to finish the course. Won't we, John?"

In the darkness John was carefully pouring cocoa into the mugs. For a moment he said nothing.

"I — don't — know," he said slowly, at last.

"*John!*" Ann was shocked. "It was you who wanted to help Ilonka! You *said* we'd got to see it through!"

"Yes, but this is different," mumbled her brother. "We didn't bargain for murders and Soviet agents. When I saw this gray-haired bloke this evening I could tell he was dangerous — "

"You saw him?" Ann and Ilonka exclaimed together.

"Yes. And got chased. I'd better tell you."

He described the encounter in Yspytty Ifan and his escape tactics after it. Ann could feel Ilonka's body growing tense against hers.

"John is right," said the Hungarian girl quietly when he had finished. "One of my enemies is close on my tail. For all I know the other — the police — may be closing in, too. It's too dangerous for you, and I ought to have thought of that before. Tomorrow you can show me on the map which way to go, and I'll leave you. I wouldn't have got this far if you hadn't helped me, but now I'll go on alone and — "

"Hold on," John cut in gruffly. "I was just considering aloud. In my opinion, Ilonka, you've got roughly ten times more chance of delivering that packet if we come with you. So we'll come, if you don't mind."

"But John!" exclaimed Ilonka.

"Hurrah!" Ann cried. "D'you know," she added, "I was beginning to think you'd been frightened off it."

"I was, nearly," John admitted. "But one has to balance these things up. I do hate leaving a job unfinished — and besides, it's the sort of adventure we might never have again. That, in my opinion, cancels out being frightened." He held out the two mugs. "It's pretty hot, but you can sip it. Here's to a safe — and secret — journey tomorrow!"

The stars winked knowingly through the branches of the rowans as they drank that toast.

# The Blondin Act

THE WILD MOORLAND Migneint Plateau
stretches from above Bala for twelve miles
to the deep Vale of Festiniog that runs down
to the sea. A few sheep graze on the craggy
hills above the bogs, but no other living thing
moves on the trackless expanse except the
grouse and the mountain hare. The one road
that crosses the plateau is the unfenced road
running southwest across a 1,600-foot pass
from Yspytty Ifan. It is a narrow ribbon
curling on the hillside close above the miniature gorge where the Conway River tumbles
over a succession of waterfalls. The tourists
who venture over the Migneint road in August very rarely discover the waterfalls, for

they are completely invisible below the steep sides of their little gorge.

The cold of a clear October morning had not yet been lessened by sunrise when John wormed his way out of the waterfall gorge and crawled up the grass slope above. Fifty feet of crawling brought him to the verge of the unfenced road, and here he stopped, lying flat with his head in a clump of rushes to listen. The morning was perfectly still. The muffled bumbling of the torrent sounded faintly below him; from the moors above the road came the distant call of a curlew. There was no sound of an approaching car, either from the valley or from the pass higher up. John put two fingers in his mouth and whistled shrilly, and in half a minute Ann and Ilonka had crawled up to lie beside him. There was still no sound of an engine, so at John's signal they rose and dashed across the road. The heathery slope on the other side was steep, but they took it at top speed and vanished over its rim.

The point where the fugitives crossed the road was six miles from Ysptty Ifan and they had taken three hours to get there. Everything had been got ready for a very early start and John, who had passed a cold night under his inadequate layer of jackets, had roused the camp with hot cocoa at half past four. By five they were away, glad of the fast going which warmed them in ten minutes. It was almost pitch-dark. John led straight down to the river by the route he had followed the previous night. He knew that there were nearly always little paths, made by trout fishermen, along the banks of mountain streams like the upper Conway River, and they did indeed find a path of sorts here and there; but it was impossible to go fast when they were dodging around boulders or through thickets most of the time. They were moving up the true right bank of the stream, with the road often only a stone's throw away above the opposite bank. A car with unusually powerful headlights passed, heading up the valley, when they had been going for an hour, and John — who was taking no chances today — made them lie flat as soon as he heard it coming, in case the reflection of the headlights should pick out their faces or shapes. It zoomed on up the hill and the three got up and resumed their half-blind progress. John thought it was too large and powerful to be the green Morris convertible; he had the impression that it was about the size and type of the usual police car. But he kept his thoughts to himself.

Dawn had come when they reached a stream coming in from the south and had to

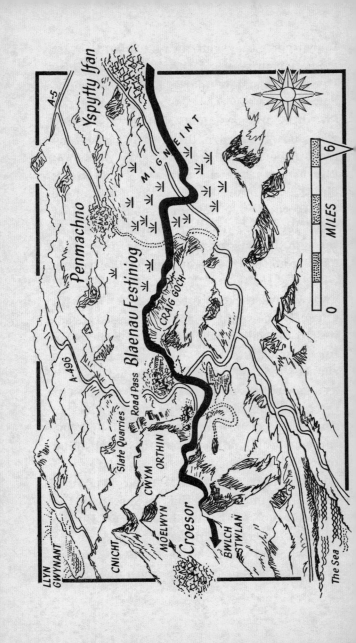

cross it by leaping perilously from rock to rock. It was just light enough now to see the map, and while John consulted it and announced their route they had a quick snack of cookies and chocolate. Once they had got across the road, said their leader, they would go a quarter of a mile due north across the moorland and then strike due west. There was a track to cross, and then open hills for four miles — a complicated system of ridges and little lakes and bogs by which, steering northwest, they could get around the slate quarrying town of Blaenau Festiniog and strike the 1,300-foot road pass two miles north of it. That road, John said, was their last real danger, for beyond it they would be among the wild mountains whose seaward-jutting spurs were the Moelwyn peaks and the mighty mountain of Cnicht. And in the valley between Moelwyn Mawr and Cnicht was the tiny hamlet of Croesor.

"It sounds an awful long way," Ann said, peering closely at the map. "And it looks it, too. Can't we shorten it?"

"Yes. We could halve the distance — by going straight down off the moors into Blaenau Festiniog and up over the Moelwyns." John folded the map and put it away. "That's out, Ann. In my opinion it would be a thundering big risk."

"And in mine," Ilonka agreed. "My ankle's in fine form — blessings on that fat woman! — and I feel I could go on walking forever on a morning like this." She sighed. "How I wish I could walk over the hills for fun instead of being hunted across them!"

"You will one day," John prophesied, shouldering his knapsack. "Let's get weaving. There's a tricky bit coming now."

It had been tricky because there was so little cover. No trees, not even a bush, broke the vast up-slope of hillside with its yellow-brown grasses brightening in the growing light. Above them, as they crept around the rocky corner where the two streams met, the deep groove cut by the Conway came zig-zagging down with the narrow road curving above its left bank. John kept along the bed of the gorge, where they were quite hidden from the road; and this several times involved them in something very like rock climbing up the sides of the little waterfalls, and more than once proved so difficult that they had to clamber along the grassy walls of the groove. All three of them had been glad to escape and get across the road at last.

Once they were up the heathery bank above the river, the road was forgotten. It was lost below them as if it had never been, and in front the wide and colored spaces of high moorland slanted gently up to the horizon without so much as a stone wall to spoil their freedom. John marched, compass in hand, at a fast pace for a good four minutes and then headed left at right angles to his original course. The sun topped the eastern hills a moment later and set the rich browns and greens of the landscape glowing. Off to their right on a stony brow a dozen specks of russet-brown drifted away like wind-blown leaves to vanish in a hollow of the moor.

"Wild ponies," John commented; and added, "There's the track — and the crest we're making for."

Right ahead the plateau of moorland rose steeply to a crinkled rim of hills. The ground in between was blotched with the bright green of bog holes and the weird black shapes of peat hags, and by the time they had crossed it they were soaked to the knees. The rough track ran along its farther side and they could see on their right the deep valley of Penmachno into which it dropped.

"We'll see the sea from that crest," John panted as they toiled up the drier hillsides beyond the track. "It's called Craig Goch — the Red Crag."

The crest had passed from sight behind

nearer hill shoulders while they were crossing the bog. Suddenly, breasting a short rise of heather, they saw it again, now quite close. And it was a strange sight.

Through the crinkles of the ridge a dense snow-white vapor was rolling, oozing slowly down the flank toward them like half a dozen avalanches in slow motion. It was as if a sea of clouds had been dammed up behind the ridge of Craig Goch and was now bursting through the dam. As they looked, they saw the white mist curl over the highest point of the crest, hiding it from view.

"Good grief!" exclaimed John. "That's a sea mist drifting up from the Festiniog valley — just when we're coming to the trickiest part of the route." He glanced behind him at the crystal-clear landscape to eastward. "It's good-bye to all that, for an hour or so anyway."

Ten minutes later they were enveloped in the white vapor. It could not have been very thick overhead, for the sunlight struck into it and made it dazzlingly bright, but that made no difference to the density of the mist that was like a moping wall always six paces in front of them as they climbed the shaly slopes to the crest.

"Stop there!"

John, a little ahead of the girls, had halted

suddenly on the brink of a sheer drop. At their feet splintered red precipices fell into mist-filled space. He backed away before consulting his compass and moving off to the right along the undulations of the crest. A few yards of sparse heather with shaly patches between the growth was all they saw now for a long time. John told the girls to keep close behind him and led them over the roughest ground they had yet encountered — up little slopes of red scree where the stones slithered away under their boots, down ledges of crumbling rock that made Ann wonder anxiously if they were actually on the face of that awesome precipice they had glimpsed. But the crest ran almost straight, south to north, and John kept his eye on the compass. At the brink of an apparently bottomless descent he stopped to check their direction with map and compass, and recheck it, before starting down a series of rock ledges draped with heather into the emptiness of the mist. It was a slightly frightening experience, and Ann heard Ilonka gasp with relief when a final slimy little wall landed them on a slope of grass. At the bottom of this the ground rose again through tall heather, fell steeply to a level of bright-red bog, rose again in more heather. It was difficult to steer a straight course over terrain that seemed to consist of little conical hills sticking up out of a marsh. They had been groping their way up and down, with the mist making them feel they were blindfolded, for what seemed a long time when Ilonka spoke suddenly.

"I'm sure we're walking around in a circle," she declared.

"So would I be if I hadn't been watching the compass," John told her, halting. "But we're not, you can take it from me. The thing is" — he hesitated — "can anyone tell me how long we've been going since crossing that track?"

"An hour," Ann guessed.

"An hour and a half at least," corrected Ilonka.

"But you don't know for sure — or do I." John got the map out of his pocket again. "I was a fool not to make a note of the time. The ground's been falling for the last few hundred yards, and if Ilonka's right we've held on too long on this northerly course — we're coming down into the head of Cwm Penmachno."

"And that's a bad thing to be doing?" queried Ilonka.

"Well, of course it is!" He snapped the words out because he was getting worried. "If we get off course to one side or the other, we're sunk. We're doing a sort of Blondin act."

"Blondin?" Ann repeated. "Wasn't he a tightrope walker?"

"Yes. Crossed Niagara Falls on a tightrope, blindfolded. These hills are the watershed between Liverpool Bay and Cardigan Bay, and I'm trying to follow the watershed until it drops to the pass where the road crosses it. And I'm blindfolded like Blondin. The difference is, that if we step off *our* tightrope we won't know it until we're down in the wrong valley — because the rope curves about instead of being dead straight like Blondin's. We should have turned west-northwest two miles after we struck Craig Goch," he added, frowning over the map.

"We must have come that far at least," Ann said. "It's ages since we were on Craig Goch."

"All right, then." John stuck the map in his pocket with an air of finality. "We'll strike west-northwest now — and let's hope we're right."

He consulted his compass carefully and then started off again, bearing to the left across the stony slope that fell away into invisibility on their right. The girls followed, Ann keeping three paces behind Ilonka. Even at that short distance the figure in front of her looked blurred and dim, so thick was the white mist. The exhilaration of the bright morning had gone and she felt anxious and miserable, partly because of the dense whiteness that pressed around them like prison walls and partly because she knew John was uncertain of the way. She had great faith in her brother's skill in route finding, which had been proved on their holiday tramps over misty hills more than once; but she knew that once you lose your position on the map, the compass ceases to be much use.

After ten minutes of awkward going over the slope, which was broken by sudden little gullies and wet shaly rocks, John began to head downhill again. He was still steering west-northwest, but the slope was curving away to the left. They wallowed through a boggy flat, crossed a faint track that was marked with pieces of slate stuck upright in the marsh, and came to another downhill slope. It dropped to a stream that flowed to the left through bushes of sweet-scented bog myrtle. They could hear the stream splashing over a waterfall a few yards away, beyond the blank curtain of mist. On the other side the ground rose steeply again, this time slanting up to the right. They topped a heathery brow and found themselves on the verge of another drop — a very steep slope of scree which fell out of the clouds into a caldron of vapor down on the left. John hesitated a moment, then clambered down the heather onto the scree and started to stamp his way across it. Ilonka followed bravely, though she was obviously frightened at the way the tiny fragments of slate slithered down under her boot soles. They had gone fifty or sixty feet across the scree when a tilted gray bar loomed out of the whiteness in front, a shadowy edge as straight as if it had been ruled across the mist at an angle of forty-five degrees. A few yards more and they could see that it was a wall or causeway built of stone blocks — but who would build a causeway like this up a mountainside? When John had climbed the six feet of inward-leaning blocks, the mystery was solved. Down the top of the causeway ran a narrow-gauge rail track, built so that trucks laden with slate could descend the incline by means of a wire hawser.

"Disused," John said, pointing to the rusty rails and rotting sleepers. "Lots of disused slate quarries around here."

He tried to sound confident, but Ann knew he was puzzled. Beyond the incline the scree slope went on, but they had not gone a dozen paces across it before it became even steeper, little rock walls fringed with parsley fern taking the place of the scree. It was really dangerous ground, either to move across or to climb up; so John backed away from it and started straight down a shallow gully at the side to look for an easier crossing. Soon the angle eased and they began to cross the slope. Up to this moment the crunch of their feet on the scree had been the only sound in an uncanny stillness. But now, from the mist-filled void below them, came the clear note of a car's horn. It sounded quite close.

John halted. "Could be the road pass," he muttered. "But the map doesn't mark any disused quarries above that. Better move on a bit."

"We can't," Ilonka said quietly. "There's an enormous cliff right in front — look!"

The whiteness around them seemed to have grown brighter, which made the huge shadow that towered above look all the darker. John moved a pace or two forward, peering at it.

"It's a slate-quarry dump," he said. "Hundreds of feet high. We know we can't climb up this slope, and I'm not going to try going back the way we've come. We'll have to get around the bottom of it."

He started down the slope, picking a way through broken fragments of slaty rock. A wind stirred the white vapor, and patches of darker hue appeared and disappeared below them.

"The mist's thinning!" Ann cried suddenly. "I saw a house then — and there's a man with a dog down there!"

It was the ghost of a house, apparently built on the floor of shifting mist. The man was walking along a path just above it, with a greyhound at his heels. He was short and wore a cloth cap, and for one sickening moment Ann was sure he must be one of the two Soviet agents and had tracked them down. Then John, who was in front and nearer the man, shouted a Welsh "good morning" at him and she knew he couldn't be an enemy.

*"Bore da!* Is there a road at the bottom of this slope?"

The man halted and stared up at them. "A road?" he repeated. "It's Blaenau High Street, man! Straight on down and you'll come to it."

With that, he whistled to the dog and walked on, passing from sight around the bottom of the slate dump. John turned a very worried face to the girls.

"We're practically in Blaenau Festiniog," he muttered. "Good grief, what a frightful mess-up! Listen — you can hear the traffic.

We must have altered course too soon instead of too late — "

"Look!" shouted Ann. "Look — *oh, look!*"

When you are in the circle of a theater and the curtain goes up, you see the feet of the people on the stage and then their arms and heads, and finally the whole stage setting is revealed. It was like that now, except that the curtain rose more slowly.

Smoothly and silently the white screen of mist lifted its bottom edge from the slope below them and went on rising. The three watchers halfway up the slope felt a strange mixture of emotions — relief and fear and excitement — as the country into which they were descending showed itself bit by bit. First the solitary house they had seen, with rows of houses below it like steps on the hillside; then a street flanked by more houses and shops and a green bus crawling past parked cars; then more houses spreading into a wide valley with a lake about a mile away; and lastly, towering beyond the lake and not far from it, a rank of splendid mountains with sunlight on their summits and sharp blue shadows marking the folds and crags of their flanks.

"The sea!" Ann exclaimed, pointing to the left.

And there it was, a narrow gleam of blue

framed in the sides of a twisting valley that ran down to southwestward. The last fringes of the mist cloud vanished overhead, leaving a blue sky flecked with white clouds. After the long hours of blank whiteness the blues and golds and distance-purples of the landscape looked incredibly bright.

"I've botched it properly," John confessed, with a miserable glance at Ilonka. "We're practically in Blaenau Festiniog. No use saying I'm sorry. We'll just have to go back, if we can find the way we — "

"I'm not going back," Ilonka said definitely; she was gazing at the shining rank of mountains. "Isn't that the pass we have to cross to get to Croesor?"

She pointed to a deep saddle toward the left end of the range between the two highest summits; the short pale-gray line of a large wall or dam showed on the mountainside below it.

"You could get to Croesor that way," John told her. "The pass is called Bwlch Stwlan — 'bwlch' means a pass — and there's a small lake with a dam, which you can see. But the shortest way is by the track up Cwm Orthin, which you can't see from here."

"Either way, we've got to go through this Blaenau place?"

"Couldn't avoid it. Unless we go back to the ridge where we were. And I suppose it's possible the ridge is still in the mist, because it's a thousand feet — "

"That settles it!" Ilonka cried almost gaily. "You said it was a thundering big risk — but this is only a little town, after all. We can walk out of it in ten minutes, and anything's better than that awful mist. Come on!"

She was off before they could stop her, plunging down the slope toward the path the man had been using. After a second's hesitation John and Ann followed. They left the solitary house a hundred yards on their left, crossed the rough path and took a lesser track that wound boggily down some grassy terraces. The rows of cottages below showed a gap, a narrow paved alley dropping straight to the street at the bottom. They flew down it in Ilonka's wake. A truck rumbled past the foot of the alley when they were nearly down. But the first person they saw — and they were only six paces from the street when they saw him — was a police constable.

# Hounds on the Scent

THE POLICEMAN WAS walking slowly along the opposite pavement, going from right to left. Ilonka tried to check her headlong pace when she saw him but only succeeded in reaching the bottom of the alley in three ungainly leaps. John and Ann, arriving simultaneously, clutched at her to stop her from falling. The helmeted head turned. The policeman directed a frowning glance at these unruly English hikers. Then he continued his stately pacing, looking straight in front of him.

"Turn right!" hissed John. "And don't hurry until we're around that bend in front!"

There were few people about on High

Street of Blaenau Festiniog, for it was ten past twelve and many of the shops were closed for lunch hour. It was a curious main street. Shops stood along it on either hand, but ahead, where it curved to the left, a vertical precipice towered above the roofs of the shops, its sheer rock walls glowing in the sunshine.

When they had gone twenty paces along the narrow pavement John glanced over his shoulder. The constable had stopped and turned. He was staring after them, with one hand raised to his chin.

"Step on it!" John muttered urgently. "Long strides."

He looked back again as they reached the bend in the street. The policeman was walking in their direction, and walking fast.

"All right — *run!*"

At John's sharp order they all broke into a trot, dodging around three elderly women gossiping in cheerful Welsh. John took the lead and quickened the pace. In a dozen yards they came to a side road on the left, with a sign on the corner in Welsh and English:

I'R YSPYTTY
HOSPITAL

John swerved left and dashed down the side

road. Behind him Ilonka was gasping something about going to that Spitty place again, but before she had got the last word out John had twisted to the left a second time. He had made a lightning calculation of the policeman's speed and the distance he had to cover, and concluded that this turning would put them out of sight just before their pursuer turned the corner. What he had not forseen was that the turning was a blind alley. It ran along the backs of four houses and ended in a blank wall. There was no way out.

They would have been caught there and then but for a lucky chance — it was trash-collection day. The back door of the houses opened on the alley and outside each door was a trash can. The girls scarcely needed John's frantic whisper of *"Take cover!"* A second after their realization that they were trapped in a dead end they were both crouching behind cans, feeling twice their proper size and quite certain that parts of them were sticking out in full view. Fortunately Ann, who was nearest the entrance of the alley, had the largest of the four trash cans and was well hidden. John was on his knees bent behind the innermost can. By pressing his bent head against the house wall he could look between the can and the wall and see the street beyond. He saw the constable run past with one quick glance up the alley. The sound of his pounding footsteps died away.

"Stay put!" John said hoarsely. "He'll be back."

The constable was sure to return as soon as he discovered that they were not in front of him. He was sure, John told himself despairingly, to pry into every side turning. And here they were, stuck because he'd tried that corny old game of doubling on his tracks again. He waited tensely and gloomily for those pounding steps to come back.

It seemed hours before he heard them coming. He braced himself for discovery. But he saw, through his spy hole, the policeman running straight past toward High Street, without a glance at the alley. As he ran he was fumbling in the breast pocket of his uniform.

John was on his feet and creeping to the mouth of the alley the moment the constable had passed. Peering around the corner, he saw the dark blue uniform speed around to the left, into High Street. A few seconds afterward there came to his ears the shrill blasts of a police whistle.

"What's that for?" demanded Ilonka from behind him.

"Summoning help — patrol car somewhere handy, like as not. Come on — and keep as close as you can."

He started running to the left, away from High Street, with the girls at his heels. They crossed a humped bridge — over a single-track railway, John noticed — and beyond it found themselves out of sight of High Street. There were any number of side alleys and back lanes in this maze of typical quarry town houses; no doubt the constable had decided it was no use trying to search them all without help. John ran straight on for a minute or so. Occasionally he glimpsed the tops of mountains above the chimney pots — they were heading too far to the left and must turn right soon if they were to reach the foot of the pass over to Croesor. He could picture the map clearly: there was a village called Tan-y-grisiau — he thought that was the name — only a mile from Blaenau Festiniog, and that was where the tracks started up over the pass. It was a mountain track and cars couldn't follow them on it. They must get to it before they were caught by police cars — or by a green Morris convertible.

An old man limping along with a stick turned and stared as the three ran past him. Ahead of them a neat white hospital appeared beyond a crossroads. John turned right at the crossroads and ran on between new-looking houses, with no one in sight except a cat who bounded out of their way with its tail in the air. The girls were keeping up well in spite of their jogging knapsacks, but though he knew Ann was a good runner, he was afraid Ilonka would have to give in soon. Then a new anxiety took the place of that one — the road was curving to the right. In the distance ahead he could see the dark face of the slate quarries — and now the sunlit precipice was coming into sight. At this rate they would soon be back on High Street again!

John looked desperately for an escape road to the left. The mountains, the blue and gold Moelwyns, rose on that side looking higher and nearer than before; but the fugitives were cut off from them by a maze of houses and gardens. And then he spied a lane forking to the left across open fields, and turned into it without slackening speed. It was short, leading into a broad new road with few houses along it which ran straight toward the mountains. They were almost at the new road when Ilonka's gasping cry reached him.

"I can't — keep up!"

John slowed to a fast walk. As they emerged onto the road he glanced to the right, half expecting to see a police car or a green Morris speeding toward them. There was a car coming, but it was a dingy-looking truck with three men in the driver's cab. On a sudden impulse he made the hitchhiker's sign with his thumb, and rather to his surprise the truck slowed up and stopped a few yards ahead. John ran after it. A young man with a mop of black hair stuck his head out.

"Only goin' to Tan-y-grisiau," he said. "There's no road beyond there."

He was looking at Ilonka, who was panting for breath with a hand on Ann's shoulder and her bright hair in a wild tangle.

"That'll do us," John said. "Can we get aboard?"

"Okay — jump in the truck. Where you bound for?"

John only hesitated for a second, but in that second a plan formed in his mind.

"Croesor," he said. "Over the pass from Cwm Orthin."

"Oh, ah," said the black-haired youth. "We're goin' to Tan-y-grisiau post office. The path goes up into the mountains from there. Get in, and look slippy 'cos I want my lunch."

The three scrambled into the back of the

truck, which was empty except for a pile of dirty sacks.

"Why on earth did you *tell* him?" Ann demanded as they started with a jerk.

Her brother didn't reply. He was standing up in the jolting vehicle, staring eagerly at the barrier of mountains that stood higher against the sky every second. Once and again he looked behind, but the wide gray road was empty of pursuit. His thoughts were working at top speed on his plan.

It was of course impossible for Ilonka to escape the police altogether. The most John could hope for was to reach Croesor before they were overtaken by their pursuers. What would happen after she had handed over the precious packet to Gyula Zichy he could not guess, but it would be up to Gyula Zichy then, police or no police. Croesor was only five miles from Tan-y-grisiau, two hours' hard going over a 1,500-foot mountain pass. With Ilonka already tired, the men who were hunting them would catch them on the Croesor path even if the fugitives got a long start — and John was only too certain that they would get very little start. A police patrol car might overtake the truck at any moment. The alarm had been given ten minutes ago, and the delay in pursuit probably meant that the police were making sure their quarry wasn't still lurking in the back streets of the town. In a matter of minutes they would pick up the trail to Tan-y-grisiau, and there they would quickly learn that a boy and two girls, one of them with long fair hair, had gone up the mountain path toward Croesor; they had only to question the men in this truck, for instance, who seemed to be staying in Tan-y-grisiau for lunch. Therefore — and this was the basis of John's plan — they must not go to Croesor by the mountain path.

The truck swung sharp right into another new-looking road. Over to the left John glimpsed a dam and a big lake, with the mountains rising steeply behind and dwarfing the raw concrete of some modern buildings. He dropped down on the pile of sacks and hurriedly consulted the map. Yes — this new road was part of the recent hydro-electric construction connected with the other dam high up under Bwlch Stwlan. The map marked a track or road — probably a road — climbing the mountainside to the dam and lake, Llyn Stwlan. A car could get up there, because the road would have been made for the trucks taking up building materials. But it looked as if the little lake, and the pass between the two Moelwyn peaks, could be reached across the open mountainside above that road —

He became aware that the truck was climbing a hill in low gear. In a few seconds it swung left and stopped in the narrow street of a small village.

"Tan-y-grisiau," said the black-haired young man, appearing at the side of the truck. "There's your track, up the hill opposite. Maybe you'd like to come in for a snack," he added with a glance at Ilonka. "My mum keeps the post office — "

"No, thanks very much." John was helping the girls down from the truck. "We're in a hurry — and we do appreciate the lift."

The truck had stopped outside a tiny post office. On the other side of the road a lane climbed very steeply above the cottages, which were perched like swallows' nests along the eaves of a mountainside. The three lost no time in starting up the lane. They passed a chapel and then one or two cottages, after which the lane became a rough track winding unfenced across a rocky slope. Overhead on their right, above ugly steeps of slate debris, crags walled in one side of the narrowing glen into which they were climbing; on the left a rank of precipices stretched away, giant buttresses supporting the eastern flank of the Moelwyns. John was setting a steady pace, and Ilonka kept close at his heels. The brief rest in the truck seemed to have done her good. A waterfall plunging over a wall of rock marked the entrance of a gorge that twisted between dark crags. The track, paved with uneven slate slabs, climbed steeply into the gorge, with the stream rushing down on its left. John's eager gaze began to search the broken cliffs that fell on this side from a crest far above, noting the broad shelves of grass and heather that slanted across them.

"Listen!" Ann said suddenly, and they all stopped.

Only a few yards of the track below them were in sight, for they had climbed well inside the narrows of Cwm Orthin. But they could hear, even above the tumult of the stream, the tread of many feet coming up the path.

"This'll have to do us. Come on — quick!"

As he spoke, John started to scramble down to the stream.

Ann began to protest that this wasn't the way, but Ilonka caught her arm and they both plunged recklessly down the bank, to leap across the torrent by way of two slippery rocks. John was already toiling up the other side. A sheer black crag towered right overhead, with a steep ledge slanting up to the left at its foot. Climbing between huge gray boulders and up wet gullies, using hands and feet and elbows in a frantic upward rush, the girls followed their leader's route toward the ledge. They were panting as if their lungs would burst when a last desperate haul brought them over a heathery edge, and both were very glad to follow John's example and fall flat behind two or three big rocks that stood on the outer edge of the shelf.

They reached this lofty hiding place with less than five seconds to spare. The track mounting from the waterfall could be seen below them, and peering down through the fringe of heather they saw five men come quickly into sight around a corner. Four of them were in uniform — three police constables and an inspector. The fifth was a tall thin man wearing a soft hat and carrying a raincoat slung over his shoulder. They climbed the rough path in single file at a very fast pace, passed the spot where the three had left the track to cross the stream, and clattered on without a single upward glance at the crags on their left. In half a

minute they were out of sight and in another
half minute the noise of their boots could no
longer be heard.

Ann sat up and frowned at her brother.
For the moment her faith in his route finding was shaken.

"It was silly to try this old dodge again,"
she said severely. "Look what you've done.
They're in front of us now, so we can't go
on. And there's nowhere else to go —"

"Yes, there is. This is a different dodge."
John pushed his crumpled map under her
nose. "We don't go on — we go around. See
this lettering, *Ceseiliau Moelwyn?* That
means 'the bosom of Moelwyn,' and it's a
sort of terrace right across below the upper
peaks to the other pass, Bwlch Stwlan."

"Is that the saddle I saw when the mist
lifted?" Ilonka asked.

"That's it. I think we can get up from this
ledge, and if we can it's perhaps half an hour
to Bwlch Stwlan. Once we're on the pass,
Croesor's only two miles away and all downhill. Think you can make it?"

"I *will* make it!" she declared, tilting her
chin resolutely.

John put his map away. "Good. Let's get
weaving, then. They can't catch us even if
they pick up our trail, but we may have to

dodge a bit to get to Gyula Zichy's cottage."

He led the way up the heathery ledge, which opened onto a boggy slope beyond a corner of the rock face. Five minutes of up-hill slogging on this, with the crags on their right continuously falling back on that side, brought them out on a wide plateau of marsh rising gently in front. John took a course that skirted the marsh, keeping on the drier slopes that dropped from the mountain ridge on their right hand. It was a place utterly quiet and apart, for a low rim of rocks on the far side of the plateau, to eastward, hid the town and its ugly quarries and showed only the crests of the far mountains they had crossed in the mist that morning. Presently the rugged east face of Moelwyn Mawr rose on their right front, with a weird-looking precipice looming beyond it. In twenty min-utes they had mounted to an old track run-ning across below the splintered crags, and almost at once Llyn Stwlan appeared far down below them in a cliff-encircled hollow — a little round lake that had once been beautiful but now was spoiled by a big gray-ish-white dam across its outer side. They could see a road climbing in tight gray coils up the precipitous mountainside below the dam.

They were halfway along the track, and directly above the lake, when Ann declared that she could hear a car. They could all hear it, in fact — the deep buzz of an engine in low gear, loudening and fading as the car twisted up the steep road to the dam. John began to make a faster pace. It was not easy to go quickly because now the old track was broken away at intervals and they had to scramble across the gaps on slopes of crumbling rubble.

But they had not much farther to go to Bwlch Stwlan. A last precarious crossing of scree, a short ascent of a grass slope, and the mountain wall on their right fell back like an opening door. They climbed into the narrow saddle of the pass, with the weird-looking precipice towering on one side and fantastic crags rising overhead on the other. The final rise of stony turf opened a tremendous view in front of them to westward.

The ground slanted steeply down from their feet to a wild glen and then, far below, opened in a distant valley where a river wound its way to the sea. The afternoon sunlight brightened the brown and gold of the nearer mountainsides to contrast with the blue glitter of the sea and the shadowed purples of the hills beyond the valley. The splendor of this sight, from the last hill crossing of their long and difficult journey, might well have held the three travelers motionless with wonder.

They were indeed held motionless, rigid as statues on the rim of the pass. But not with wonder. Coming up from the other side of the pass, fifty paces away, were two men. One of them was a little man wearing a cloth cap. The other was much taller, with no hat on his fine mane of gray hair.

# Showdown on the Pass

THE TWO MEN had stopped dead when the others appeared so suddenly on the pass just above them. Now they came on up the stony slope. The gray-haired man had a pair of binoculars slung over his shoulders. His small companion, a pace behind him, kept one hand in the pocket of his short jacket.

Every mystery story he had read about secret agents and their ways seemed to flash through John's mind. He looked wildly to left and right for a chance of escape and found no hope in the bare crag-topped slopes on either side of the pass. Down the side they'd come up, then — there was cover among the rocks.

"Get back, quick!" he yelled at the girls. "Come on!"

"*Stop!*" Ilonka almost spat the word at him. "It's no good, John," she added in a shaky voice. "He's got a gun."

A small black automatic pistol had appeared in the little man's hand, and it was pointed at John. The tall man barked an order at him in a foreign language and he shrugged and returned the pistol to his pocket. As they continued to advance, the tall man spoke loudly to Ilonka, again in a foreign language. The Hungarian girl lifted her chin defiantly.

"My friends don't understand Hungarian," she replied; and now her voice was clear and steady. "If I must talk to you, it will be in English or not at all."

"Very well," said the tall man.

He halted six feet in front of Ilonka, who had slipped her knapsack from her shoulders and taken a step forward so that John and his sister were behind her. Ann moved closer to John. She was very frightened, but even in her fright she could not help thinking that the gray-haired man didn't look a bit like a ruthless Soviet spy; his fine hawk-like face, brown and crinkly, was much too distinguished-looking. Though he was gazing very sternly at Ilonka, he looked as if he were more often kind than merciless. She noticed, too, a sort of likeness in the two erect figures confronting each other.

"I will be brief." The tall man's deep voice was deadly serious. "I am Ferenc Dayka. My comrade here is Janos Zemlenyi. He is armed, as you have seen."

The little man wriggled his hand in the pocket of his jacket and nodded.

"But we shall, I hope, avoid any kind of violence," continued Ferenc Dayka steadily. "We know that you are Ilonka Kazinczy, we know that you are carrying papers, or a book, to the cottage of Gyula Zichy at Croesor village. You will not deny this?"

"I will say nothing," said Ilonka flatly.

John could almost feel her willing him to act. Her knapsack lay on the ground behind her, a foot from his toes, and the packet was in the knapsack.

"Then I must do the talking," Ferenc said with a little shrug. "We have followed you from London, Miss Kazinczy. Janos was watching your uncle's house when you came out, shortly after Zoltan Melich was killed."

Ilonka's eyes flashed. "Then it was Janos who murdered Uncle Zoltan!" she cried accusingly. "Janos or you! How else could you have known — "

"That is a lie, Miss Kazinczy!" Ferenc's steel-gray eyes gleamed as fiercely as the girl's. "Janos had followed a certain man — one of us — who was known to have sworn Melich's death. He saw him go into the house, and waited — "

"He could have stopped him!"

"He did not do so. Nor did Janos make any move when he saw this man drop from a window and escape. The deed was justified, Miss Kazinczy. Your uncle, as you must know, was an evil man, a traitor, a blackmailer, a — " he broke into a torrent of rapid Hungarian.

John had listened with only half an ear. He had decided that Ilonka wanted him to take the packet from her knapsack if he could. There was no hope of hiding it from Ferenc and Janos, but the alternative — to destroy it before they could lay hands on it — might just be possible, and was certainly the only thing to do now. But it would be very difficult to do that while the gloomy gaze of Janos Zemlenyi was fixed on them, as it was now.

Ferenc was speaking English again. "I tell you that what Zoltan Melich and Gyula Zichy were doing is a black crime — in England as anywhere. Listen. When Janos and I failed to catch you and take the papers, we went straight to Croesor. We were sure you must be taking them to Gyula and we had discovered his address. We intended to give him a thrashing and tie him up, then wait for you at his cottage. What happens? We arrive at Croesor this morning and we are told Gyula Zichy has been arrested. The police had taken him away."

"The police arrested him?" Ilonka said blankly. "But . . . why?"

"For blackmail, doubtless," Ferenc told her grimly. "He and Melich were partners in a business so dirty, so vile, that — "

Again he went off into angry Hungarian. John spoke to Ann in an urgent whisper, from the corner of his mouth.

"Rock twenty paces on our left. Walk to it and sit on it. You're tired, can't stand. Stay there as long as you can. Get weaving!"

Ann knew from his tone that this was important. She obeyed at once, turning away and walking to the flat-topped rock with a weariness that was not at all pretense. Janos swung around and pulled the gun half out of his pocket.

"Where you go?" he demanded shrilly. "Get back with the others! You hear me?"

Ann flopped down on the rock. "But I'm

tired," she protested. "We've come an awful long way, you've no idea. We started in the dark, and then we lost our way in the mist . . . ."

Ferenc, as well as Janos, had looked away toward Ann and John hadn't missed his chance. He had stooped swiftly and picked up Ilonka's knapsack. Now he was standing with his legs apart and his hands behind his back, his fingers busy with the lacings of the sack. He grasped the packet at last. The paper wrapping was tied with string but the string felt as if it could be wriggled off. He allowed the knapsack to drop to the ground behind him.

"Let her stay there, Janos," Ferenc said impatiently, interrupting Ann's tale of woe. "And put that pistol in your pocket. You are too fond of pretending to be a gunman. Now, Miss Kazinczy, we want those papers — or whatever it is you were carrying to Gyula Zichy."

"And if I refuse to give them?"

"Then you will be a fool. You know well they hold the difference between happiness and misery — perhaps between life and death — for many Hungarians."

Ilonka frowned. "And this is why I am to give them to you, of all people?" she said incredulously.

"This is why we must take them from you." Ferenc seemed to be restraining his impatience. "I have said we do not wish violence, but if we must use force — and possibly hurt your friends — then we shall do so."

"You shall not touch my friends, Ferenc Dayka!" cried the girl fiercely. "They have nothing to do with this — they have only helped me on my journey, and bravely too."

There was a touch of playacting in her manner, and John guessed she was doing her best to give him more time. He had wriggled the string off and was stripping the wrapping paper, hoping that the rustling noise wouldn't be heard. His fingers felt a small notebook of the cheap sort, with a stiff cover. He began to wrench the pages from the cover, all the time staring at the watchful Janos and trying to look thoroughly scared. He found it easier to look scared than to loosen the pages, with his hands behind his back and without letting the sheets of paper fall. The matches, he remembered with a sudden thrill of excitement, were still in his pocket where he had put them after the early morning fire making — it seemed more like ten years ago than ten hours, that fire.

"I do not doubt these English helped you bravely," Ferenc was saying. "I will say honestly, Ilonka Kazinczy, that I admire your own courage. But bravery is worthless in an evil cause, and in your case it has been useless because Zichy is no longer there to receive the papers." He took a step forward and held out his hand. "Give them to me!"

Ilonka played her last card. "You may as well know the police are close behind us," she said desperately. "You won't get away, even if you knock us down to get what you want."

For the first time the tall man looked puzzled. His keen eyes narrowed as he studied the girl's face.

"The police!" he repeated slowly. "But it is you, not Janos and I, who have to fear the police."

John was almost ready. He was fingering the pages torn from the notebook, working out the sequence of actions he would have to perform at lightning speed when the time came. There was one instant when he hesitated, wondering at himself. He was supposed to be on a holiday tramp with his young sister, not taking part in a battle of wits between Hungarians and Soviet spies, with the British police hunting him at the same time. He looked at Ann, still sitting dejectedly on her rock. He remembered the pistol in the little man's pocket, and gulped as he thought what might happen when he made his first move. The whole thing must be a dream, a nightmare — he would wake up in a minute, or the dream would end, as such dreams often did, with help arriving unexpectedly from somewhere.

But the tang of the sea in the chill air blowing over the pass, the murmur of a stream far down in the empty glen were not the sort of thing that came to you in a dream. And there was no help in the barren mountainsides or the crags that had looked so fine when they were toiling up to the pass. The situation was real enough. He and Ann had got themselves up to the neck in Ilonka's troubles and there was no way out. He had to go through with this last desperate plan.

Ferenc was still staring at Ilonka with a puzzled frown. He rumpled his mane of hair with one hand as he went on speaking.

"It is true that we are not anxious for the police to question us. That is why we were returning by this pass from Croesor rather than by the one the police might use in their search for you — that, and because we hoped to espy you with these as you crossed the valley." He patted his binoculars. "But you reached the mountains much sooner than we expected."

He turned to Janos and they exchanged a

few words in their own language. John seized the opportunity.

"Ilonka!" he said quietly. "I'm so hot I'm *ready for burning*. I could do with a diversion, though."

Ilonka spoke without turning her head. "Good. Stand by, then."

Ferenc had swung around when he heard their murmured conversation, and the steely eyes flashed a suspicious glance at John. But he continued to speak to Ilonka.

"Janos has been in these hills before. He tells me this pass is very rarely visited. Our little talk is most unlikely to be interrupted — and indeed there has been enough talk." Again he held out his hand. "For the last time, Miss Kazinczy, I demand that you give me those papers. If you do not — *ough!*"

He ended with a gasp of surprise. Ilonka had literally hurled herself headfirst under his outstretched arm — not at him, but at Janos. John, who had launched his own mad rush as soon as she moved, saw that magnificent flying tackle from the corner of his eye and wondered confusedly whether Hungarian girls played Rugby football. The little man went down with a yell and a thud, and the two rolled wildly about in a tangle of threshing arms and legs. John didn't see this. He had reached the bare patch of scree twenty yards away and was hurriedly crumpling and setting down his pile of papers — the notebook pages covered with names and addresses and neatly penned details. He had the matches out in an instant. The thought that Janos might free himself and shoot at him set his hands shaking, but he controlled them. The papers flared as he held the match to them. Simultaneously a roar from Ferenc made him turn.

The tall man had remained motionless and speechless, as if rigid with astonishment, while John did his hasty fire raising. Now Ann had entered the fray. Charging from her boulder, she leaped bodily at Ferenc and twined her arms around his neck in a stranglehold.

"Hoi! Stop, you wildcat!" What sounded like Hungarian swear words came next. "This is all wrong! Let — me — go!"

On the last word he tore Ann's grip from him, shook her once in midair, and set her down on her feet. Then he strode quickly to the struggling pair on the ground.

"Janos, drop that gun! Ilonka Kazinczy, loose the man and get up! I must have the truth of this, here and now!"

Ilonka stood up, panting. Her tangled hair

was full of brown grass and a large bruise was developing on her cheekbone. Janos, spitting oaths and rubbing his arm, had two long red scratches down his face. He stuffed the pistol in his pocket as he got sullenly to his feet. Ann stood by tensely, apparently poised for another leap at Ferenc. Before any of them could speak, John had joined the odd little group.

"No one will ever read those names now," he said, looking at Ilonka.

On the scree behind him the fire of paper blazed high. The breeze from the distant sea caught one of the burning pages and sent it skipping over the crest of the pass, changing it into black ash as it flew. Ferenc was looking at Ilonka too, with a very curious expression. When he spoke, his deep voice had become strangely gentle.

"The names on the papers you have burned were those of the men who form our Action Group, members of Free Hungary in Great Britain. Your British friend here — he has courage enough to be a Hungarian — burned the papers to prevent them from falling into the hands of Janos and myself. You agree to this first proposition, Miss Kazinczy?"

"To prevent them from falling into the hands of the enemy!" Ilonka cried, tilting her chin defiantly. "The oppressors, the Soviets, those who sent you and this Janos man to spy on — "

She was interrupted by Janos, who started forward with waving arms and a volley of rapid Hungarian. Ferenc swept him aside with a raised arm.

"Janos' wrath must be excused," he said, in the same gentle tone. "You see, Miss Kazinczy, he and I have been hunting you for four days with the same object as your own — to prevent those lists from falling into the hands of the enemy. For Gyula Zichy, like your uncle Zoltan Melich, was a deadly enemy of Free Hungary."

Ilonka tossed her hair back from her face to stare at him uncertainly.

"I — I don't believe it!" she said. "You mean Gyula Zichy was a Soviet agent? And my uncle too?"

"They were worse than that," said the tall man gravely. "Did you not hear me call them blackmailers? Between them they ran what you would call a racket — a devilish racket. Many of those who work secretly here in Britain, against the Soviet rule, have relatives and friends in Hungary. To betray the name of such a person to an agent of Soviet Hungary would mean terrible hardship, even torture and death, for his relatives and friends in our oppressed country. Melich and Zichy had gathered by devious methods a list of our most active members, and were extorting money from them under threat of betraying them."

"But look here," John put in, "why didn't you put the police on to them? You said yourself blackmail's a black crime."

"Because the British police cannot be told of our doings. They are not — within the law, I think the phrase is. One man, who had been most sorely threatened because his wife and family were still in Hungary, took the law into his own hands and Zoltan Melich is dead. Melich might still be alive," Ferenc added thoughtfully, "had I succeeded in finding those papers when I broke into his house a fortnight ago."

"So it was you!" Ann, who had been listening intently, broke into the conversation. "It all fits in . . . . Ilonka, you believe him now, don't you? I'm absolutely sure Mr. Dayka is a good man!"

When Ferenc Dayka smiled, as he did now, his steel-gray eyes turned to dancing blue and his brown face lost all its sternness.

"I would never claim to be that, my wild-cat," he said. "I try only to work for the right. If — *istenem!*"

He jerked out the exclamation. Ilonka, without any warning, had cast herself on the ground and was sobbing as if her heart would break.

Janos bent to help her, and Ferenc assisted him to lift her to her feet. The tall man put his arm around her and she did not resist.

"You feel you have been defeated," he said quietly, "but it is not so, Ilonka. You feel you have put forth so much anxiety, and toil, and courage, all for nothing." He was leading her toward Ann's flat-topped rock as he spoke. "Between us we have won. The evil thing is destroyed."

He pointed to the smoking heap of ashes. Then, still with his arm across Ilonka's shoulders, he began to chuckle.

"Forgive me," he said, looking at the three who were staring at him. "In England I have learned to laugh at strange jokes. And surely it is a strange joke that we five should have been dodging and hiding and tracking each other across Wales — like demented Boy Scouts — when all the time we were on the same side!"

John scratched his head. "I suppose — yes, it's a joke all right," he said, and began to laugh.

Ann laughed too, out of sheer relief. Janos

Zemlenyi looked doubtfully at his chief and then emitted a shrill giggle. Ilonka, raising her head, smiled faintly through her tears at Ferenc, who was now fairly guffawing.

"And a very jolly party too!" said a booming voice from behind them.

The laughter stopped instantly and they all spun around to see a big red-faced man just reaching the top of the pass from the Llyn Stwlan side. He wore climbing boots, breeches, and an old deerstalker hat.

"Dunno if it's in order for the Special Branch to join the party," he said genially as he reached them. "But that's me — Evans, Chief Inspector."

# Journey's End

ANN was to remember afterward how Bwlch Stwlan seemed to darken at that moment, as if there were a play being acted on the pass, with stage lighting to match. The weird nose of crag high on the left and the jagged walls of the ridge opposite, the grass and rock of the saddle and the backcloth of seaward lands below — all had lost their sunlit brightness when Ferenc and Janos appeared. The autumn gold had shone once more over everything when it was discovered that they were not enemies after all. But now the gold was lead, the mountains unfriendly again. She had entirely forgotten about the police.

Chief Inspector Evans seemed not to notice the consternation his arrival had produced. Ilonka had jumped up from the rock where she had been sitting — Ann noticed she went straight to Ferenc, who put a protective arm around her — and Mr. Evans sat down on the rock with a grunt.

"Thank you, my dear," he said. "Not so spry as I was, y'know. Mind you, my wind's all right — came up from Llyn Stwlan nonstop. Grand day for the hills, eh? Years since I was on Bwlch Stwlan. I come from these parts, y'know — born in Merioneth."

As he talked in this casual way, he was filling a pipe from a battered old tobacco pouch. At the same time, his large pale blue eyes in turn surveyed each of the five who stood around him. All of them were looking apprehensive, and Janos, whose hand had gone into his pocket again, was obviously frightened. He muttered something to Ferenc in rapid Hungarian.

"And what might that mean?" inquired Mr. Evans mildly.

"He says," Ferenc answered, "that he does not believe you are really a detective policeman."

"Oh, I'm a copper all right," said the red-faced man with a beaming smile. "If you won't take my word for it, you can use those Yashica ten-by-fifties you've got slung around you — you'll see my car down by the dam, with three cops in helmets by it. I daresay I'd be in order if I asked your pal if he has a license for that gun he's got in his pocket. As for being a detective" — his pale-blue glance darted around him — "I deduce someone's been having a bit of a scrap. I won't guess why. And someone's been burning papers, not so very long ago. No doubt it's all part of your little mystery, Miss Kazinczy — eh?"

He beamed at the frightened Ilonka. Ferenc tightened his arm around the girl's shoulders.

"May I ask, sir, what you want of us?" he demanded.

"Certainly. I want Ilonka Kazinczy. Mind you" — Mr. Evans wagged a big forefinger at them — "she's not my pigeon, strictly speaking. She's a C.I.D. job. But seeing that Inspector Fosdyke's gone over the other pass on a wild-goose chase — yes, my dear?"

Ilonka had let out an exclamation. "I — I thought I recognized — " She stopped herself.

"You spotted him, then," nodded the Chief Inspector. "Yes, it was Fosdyke chasing you up Cwm Orthin with his men. It's his case, y'know, the murder of Zoltan Melich. You scuttled past him, Miss Kazinczy, on the night of your uncle's death, and told him a lie or two. Friend Fosdyke is sore about that. You've led him a fine chase — thanks to your two assistants." His gaze fixed itself on John and Ann. "Mr. John Davies and sister, I presume?"

John nodded, too nervous to speak. Ann, who was on tenterhooks, burst out suddenly.

"Why don't you tell us?" she cried angrily. "Are you going to arrest Ilonka? And us?"

"Not them!" Ilonka flashed, shaking off Ferenc's arm and stepping forward. "They didn't know — I told them I was running away from home — "

"Yes, yes, yes," said Mr. Evans soothingly. "There'll be no more arrests, far as I can see. Mind you, I'll have to take Miss Kazinczy back to London with me. Fosdyke needs her evidence, and I've no doubt she'll get a bit of a talking to for running off like that. Made us all think she had something to do with the murder, y'know, until yesterday, when this Hungarian fellow gave himself up and said he'd done it."

He struck a match and applied it to his pipe. Janos suddenly jerked out an anxious question.

"This Hungarian — he say why he kill Melich?"

Mr. Evans turned a wide stare on him and got his pipe well alight before replying.

"Listen, Mr. Who'sit," he said. "I don't want to know anything about you. Or" — he waved Ferenc into silence as he opened his mouth — "or about you, Mr. Whatnot. Understand that. I'm Special Branch, as I told you. I've been pulled in on this case because the boys up top thought it might have what they call political repercussions. But I've got enough on my plate without having to dig into whatever game you . . . er . . . aliens are playing, so keep quiet, both of you."

Ferenc drew a deep breath. "I understand, Chief Inspector. But the murder — "

"A straight case of victim killing blackmailer, far as I can see," said the Chief Inspector placidly, between puffs. "Victim put us on to Mr. Gyula Zichy, Melich's partner in the game — nasty piece of work, your uncle, Miss Kazinczy — and Zichy was arrested this morning. But I'm not being allowed to tell my tale properly."

He beamed and nodded at John and Ann, who were standing close together, both with the same expression of mingled hope and anxiety on their faces.

"I've been following your trail with interest," he continued. "On the map, of course, as reports came in. When I heard you'd left plain indication you were going to Croesor by the Cwm Orthin pass, I said to myself, 'That lad's trying to diddle us, like he did before,' I said. 'He's going some other way.' Me knowing these mountains, I reckoned it must be over Bwlch Stwlan. Fosdyke wouldn't have it, so I came up myself. It's nice to be proved right — and nicer to have an excuse for a little walk on the hills. My thanks to you, John and Ann — and congratulations on your hillcraft."

He got up and stood looking out to westward, over the falling mountainsides to the far valley and the sea. The afternoon sun was sinking toward the humped blue shapes of distant hills beyond the valley, and the wide bar of sea was glittering gold. The smoke of the Chief Inspector's pipe drifted on the sea wind, as blue as the faraway mountains.

"Pity to leave all this and go back to London," he remarked sadly. "But duty is duty, y'know. If you're ready, Miss Kazinczy . . ."

"I'm ready. But, Mr. Evans" — Ilonka hesitated — "will I be allowed to go when the police have finished questioning me?"

"Of course, my dear, though you'll be wanted later as a witness." Mr. Evans' round red face creased itself in a sudden frown and he took his pipe from his mouth. "But — where will you go? That's a point, y'know. Far as I can see, Zoltan Melich was all you had in the way of family and home."

"Chief Inspector!"

Ferenc Dayka's deep voice rang loudly as he stepped forward. With his tall, erect figure and silver-gray mane he looked, thought Ann, a great deal more distinguished than the Special Branch man.

"I shall accompany Ilonka Kazinczy to London, if you please," he continued rapidly. "She is of my own people and she has no protector. If she will make her home with me and my wife — we are childless — we shall be proud to have her. Will you do so, Ilonka?"

The light in Ilonka's eyes as she grasped the hand he held out to her was sufficient answer. Chief Inspector Evans rubbed his chin doubtfully.

"Well, I suppose that's all right," he said slowly. "Mind you, a court will have something to say when it comes to legal guardianship — "

"We will meet that problem in due course, sir." Ferenc, still holding Ilonka's hand, glanced over his shoulder at Janos. "My companion will travel with us."

"This is where you take orders from me, my lad," the Chief Inspector told him firmly. "Miss Kazinczy goes in the police car. You and that bandit of yours can follow in your own car — green Morris convertible, isn't it? We've had an eye on it, y'know. And that" — he swung around to face John and Ann — "that leaves you two."

For Ann the sunlight had come back to the pass. The crags had friendly faces again and the shadows had fled to the eastward hills where they had journeyed and hidden for four strenuous days. John, who still expected some penalty for their part in the affair, eyed the big policeman nervously.

"I've got some orders for you as well," said Mr. Evans solemnly, in his booming voice. "I'm saying nothing about your little adventure. It's over now. But — take my advice and don't help girls who are on the run from the police, even when they're as pretty as this one. As for orders, the first one's this. You'll go straight down to Croesor village, where you'll see a telephone booth. Ring up your parents and tell them all's well. The papers had your names in two days ago and they'll be worrying, y'know. Second — you're going to camp tonight?"

"Yes," John said.

"Right." He pulled a notebook from his pocket and scribbled with a stump of pencil. "Don't camp on the *traeth* — the river valley yonder — where the night mist rises and freezes you stiff. I know because I've camped there myself, years ago." He tore the page from the notebook and handed it to John. "Go to this address in Croesor and bang on the door. The chap there will tell you a good place to camp. Probably give you some tea as well, specially if you hint that you've been having an adventure of sorts. He's a book-writing chap — might make a book about *you*, for all I know. That's all. Good camping to you!"

As he turned away, Ilonka left her new guardian and ran to them. She was carrying John's sleeping bag, which had been in her knapsack.

"There isn't going to be time to thank you properly," she said breathlessly, handing over the sleeping bag. "We'll meet, won't we? And I'll write — Ann told me your address. I've" — she stopped, frowning and smiling at the same time — "it's funny, but though it was pretty awful at times, I've kind of enjoyed it all."

"So have we," John said, sounding surprised.

"Now that it's ended all right," Ann added.

"And we'll do a proper mountain walk," Ilonka hurried on. "Perhaps next spring. I'll buy myself a sleeping bag, John, and we can do another journey, without any secret next time — "

"Miss Kazinczy!" called the Chief Inspector.

Ilonka bent quickly and kissed Ann. She hesitated, and then grabbed John and kissed him too.

"Good-bye — good-bye!"

She darted away to join the three men who were waiting for her. Ferenc Dayka had her knapsack in his hand as, with Ilonka close beside him, he followed the Chief Inspector and Janos down the beginning of the descent on the east side of Bwlch Stwlan. Just before they passed from sight, Ilonka turned and waved her hand.

John, whose face was very red, took a step after them as if to watch them go all the way down to the Stwlan dam. Ann glanced at him rather anxiously.

"The adventure's over," she said quietly. "And — it's getting chilly up here. Hadn't we better get down to Croesor and find this campsite?"

"Yes," said her brother dully. "Yes, I suppose so."

He stuffed the sleeping bag Ilonka had used into his knapsack, slung the sack on his shoulders, and turned to face the western glen and the sinking sun.

"It'll be really choice if we can do a hill tramp with Ilonka next spring," Ann said. "We might even finish our beeline."

John brightened up. "That'd be pretty average good," he agreed. "It'll be funny, though, with no one chasing us . . . Good grief, it's nearly four! Come on!"

They began to walk down the seaward slopes of the pass, toward Croesor. Before they had gone twenty paces, John was whistling snatches from *"Eine Kleine*

*Nachtmusik"* and Ann was smiling contentedly to herself. Their footsteps called faint diminishing echoes from the crags that flanked the pass and then faded away altogether. Except for the whisper of the wind in the grasses and the murmur of distant mountain streams, Bwlch Stwlan was silent and lonely once again. The only sign that an adventure had ended there was a little heap of black ashes on the slope.